Copyright © 2026 Juliet Loo
All rights reserved

The characters and events portrayed in this book are fictitious. Any similarity to real persons, living or dead, is coincidental and not intended by the author.

No part of this book may be reproduced, or stored in a retrieval system, or transmitted in any form or by any means (electronic, mechanical, photocopying, recording, or otherwise), without express prior written permission of the copyright owner.

Digital ISBN: 978-0-473-77457-8
Print ISBN: 978-0-473-77458-5
978-0-473-77459-2

Blind Date Betrayal

Serena Black

By Serena Black

Ten Easy Steps
The Reluctant Bride
Leonie's Christmas Miracle
The Gift of Love

Sisters & Scoundrels
The Magic of San Miguel
Taming the Golden Dragon
The Tale of Two Bostons

For my parents,

I love you.

Chapter One

Phoenix Chan stood looking out from his office in Aurora Financial Services at the skyscape and busy streets of New York City. How long had it been since he last stopped to appreciate the view and the life he had worked so hard to achieve? Too long if he was asking himself the question.

Being the second son and fourth sibling out of six in the Chan family, there was something comforting about being not only in the middle of the pack, but the youngest son. He didn't have the same heavy burden of responsibility his eldest brother and sister did. Although, just like his older brother Boston, it didn't stop him taking his responsibilities as an elder brother to two younger sisters seriously, or even towards his elder two sisters when required. Something all his sisters had hated especially when they were younger.

Known as the family hothead when he was younger, he

was always ready to jump into the fray without thought of the situation or consequence.

These occurrences were more frequent at school as the majority of altercations involved people teasing him or his siblings about their names, and it was always Boston who was left to try and calm him down.

"Sticks and stones," Boston would say. Well, Phoenix was in complete agreement there. He'd happily beat his tormentors with a stick or throw stones at them.

The one thing which seemed to temper his fiery nature and direct it into some sort of positive outlet was sport.

Phoenix was one of those naturally talented and super sporty boys who played every sport available. He was also very competitive and found himself in more than a few heated altercations during these times as well.

However, he always left his aggression on the field of play and so fellow competitors knew Phoenix was one of those people who when the final whistle blew, could just switch off and be friends with everyone.

As he aged, he realised it was time to not only grow up, but also to try and mellow a little. Of course while he was able to occasionally be irresponsible, unfortunately these days, those times were few and far between. The only thing he really had time for besides his family and work were women. A carousel of women who also weren't into long-term relationships suited a young man perfectly and as he moved up the ladder of success, the only thing to change about the women were that they went from normal and down to earth, to more superficial, polished and preened.

Still, Phoenix found no shortage of women willing to just have fun in the sack. No strings, no promises, which meant he could continue to burn the candle at both ends without a nagging girlfriend to add to his stress.

To some, his life was perfect.

The irony of his life was that probably, like most people, he was just trying to find someone he could connect with on a more basic level, like family values, laughter and common interests. Not just in superficial terms of status, money or sex.

Yes, his bed partners were purely superficial meetings. Nothing shared was either too personal or in-depth and was either about their jobs, general chit-chit or other superficial frivolous things, just to pass the time until they got down to sex.

Phoenix couldn't tell you if the last woman he slept with was an only child, what she did besides her job or even where she grew up. None of that mattered to either party.

Releasing a long breath, he realised just how fast life was passing and apart from some very good friends and family, there was no one special in his life he could share things, love, or even relax with. He was even beginning to miss those down to earth women he once knew.

Great, now he was being contrary, not knowing what he truly wanted.

Ever since Boston, who was also his best friend, flew the nest and begun making something of himself, Phoenix too, had the urge to follow. It was also because he missed his big brother a lot. They had never been apart for such a long period and phone calls and talking over the internet wasn't the same as having your best friend around all the time.

It didn't help when Boston argued Phoenix or Nix, as he was known to his nearest and dearest, should get at least one job after leaving university under his belt in New Zealand before going over to England to do his OE — overseas experience — like lots of other Kiwis.

Phoenix chaffed at the advice.

"Seriously, it's more beneficial for you in the long run. As much as you'd happily be hired by me, or our brothers-in-law Jason or Lucas, if people knew you were related, it wouldn't really give them much confidence on whether they were being told to hire you because of nepotism or you'd actually be good at the job," Boston said.

"Fine," he grumbled, seeing the wisdom of his brother's advice.

Phoenix found himself a job in an accounting firm, as he thought being an accountant was his career calling. This stint actually led him to acknowledge he didn't enjoy accounting at all. Although he loved and had a natural talent with numbers, it wasn't until he landed his first job in England that he realised investment finance was where he wanted to be.

At the time Boston was living in New York, so when Phoenix first landed in London, he initially lived with their older sister, Indi and her husband, Jason to acclimatise to his surroundings. Not really knowing Jason since the couple lived in England while he had still been in New Zealand, Phoenix found he and Jason got on well. It was also great to be able to talk to someone like Jason about his future, as he knew Boston had done the same when he lived there.

Although Boston and Jason both knew Tony Santamaria, it was Boston who got Phoenix a job interview with him. He smiled remembering the day which started his own meteoric rise in the business world…

"So you're related to Boston and Jason," Tony smiled.

Phoenix was nervous, unsure if Tony's smile was one of condescension or friendliness.

"Y-yes," he said.

"Boston tells me you're quite the whiz with numbers and you don't want to be an accountant. Perhaps investment finance might be up your alley?" Tony said.

"I-I don't know," he said.

Tony looked at the young man sitting across from him and didn't quite know what to make of him. Phoenix's nervousness didn't help Tony to know if Phoenix was as good as his brother seemed to think. According to Boston, Phoenix had the same quick study and smart genes he did, and therefore could be someone Tony might consider mentoring. Still there was a sense of wariness that perhaps Boston had just talked Phoenix up and he wasn't as good as his brother thought.

Already knowing Boston and Jason, Tony's initial feeling was Phoenix would also be cut from the same cloth, which put Tony at ease. He was quite particular in hiring people, more so ones who were recommended to him, especially if he didn't have any open vacancies. If he received any inkling the possible future employee only wanted a job thinking it was their ticket to get rich quick or because their family or friend got the job for them, but they really didn't care about the work or industry, then those people received a polite interview ending with apologies that there were no vacancies. If on occasion he managed to find them a very junior entry job, he wouldn't mentor them in any capacity because they were the people who wouldn't value his wisdom or experience.

To try and put Phoenix at ease and to see just how capable this young man really was, Tony decided to give Phoenix a little test on something he knew one of his staff was working on.

"You don't have much career experience and none in investment finance. However, let me ask you, what you would do if our client Mr Smith wanted to…"

They chatted for over an hour and Tony found himself marvelling at the way Phoenix's mind worked. The young man may not have any real experience, but the way he processed his thoughts and questions were always instinctively right on the nose.

Tony knew right then and there, Phoenix would be his new protégé, not that he had even been looking for one. Nevertheless, his instincts screamed Phoenix was someone who he knew would go far and with the right guidance his trajectory really could be limitless.

Shortly after their interview Phoenix joined Tony at the boutique company, Guardian Investment Services where working closely together, he proved he was not only a whiz with numbers, but a very quick study. Thus it wasn't long before Phoenix was handling some of the company's major clients. Some were rightly worried, however just as Tony suspected, after Phoenix had handled their accounts, if they were offered the chance to have their account handled by someone else they never accepted. Those clients knew Phoenix would guide them onto even more untold wealth.

"Nix, you got time for lunch today?" Tony said, entering his office.

"Sure," he said, looking at his watch, seeing it was now two in the afternoon. He could use a break and enjoyed chatting to Tony.

"Great, let's go," Tony said.

They went to a little pizzeria which was now quiet since the lunch rush was over.

"I wanted you to be the first to know I've been offered a new job," Tony said.

"That's fantastic," he smiled. "Can I ask who or is it not a done deal yet?"

It was the answer Tony had come to expect from Phoenix after working so closely with him all this time. Phoenix wasn't jealous of someone else's success if they had worked hard and earned it. He was always supportive and that's why he was still in contact with a lot of the staff who had moved onto other jobs.

"It's an American company and at the moment their investment division is lagging, which is why they need a wizard like me. I'm actually going to be the new investment director when the old one retires and therefore don't officially start for a while," Tony grinned.

"Isn't this a step down for you?" Phoenix frowned.

"Yes and no. I'm looking forward to the challenge, which is what I need. Time to get out of the rut, so to speak," Tony said.

"Well, as long as you stay on your side of the pond, we're all good because I'd hate to have to take you down," he laughed.

Although happy for his friend, Phoenix was feeling a little nervous. He and Tony had worked closely together for so long, what was he going to do once his friend and mentor left? What if he didn't get on with his new boss? How was he going to manage without even the thought of having Tony as his safety net?

Sensing Phoenix's anxiety, Tony decided to put his young protégé out of his misery.

"So here's the thing, and it's something you really need to carefully consider," he said.

"What's that?" Phoenix said.

"I'm going to recommend you take over my job in London —"

"Me?" The stunned look on Phoenix's face showed he had no idea that was what Tony was about to say. "B-but I don't know how to manage a company and there's other people infinitely more qualified and experienced," he said.

"Actually you do," Tony smiled. "What do you think you've been doing all this time when people come to you for help?"

"Helping them?" he said.

The confused look on Phoenix's face made Tony laugh.

"Yes, it's also called being a manager. Everyone in the office knows if they can't get me, to go to you because you'll give them the help they need," Tony said.

"But you do all the reports and meetings and stuff," he said.

"You'll still have Linda and Sarah who know the ropes. Once this comes out, I'll be out the door if not immediately, but soon. But for you, I'll always just be a phone call away," Tony said.

Phoenix sat there in a daze. Never in his wildest imagination had he thought Tony would suggest he take over his job. He still felt like the new kid on the block in terms of experience.

"I don't know…" he said, hesitant.

"Like I said, it's something you have to think very carefully about. But there is another option," Tony smiled.

"Which is?" he said.

"I'll make it one of my conditions that you come with me to New York," Tony said.

That statement made Phoenix bug eyed while his mouth gaped open. The offer was incredible, almost beyond his wildest dreams. Then reality hit.

"Won't people think it's a bit…" He wasn't sure how to phrase the question so it didn't seem tawdry or dishonest.

"I'm not planning on installing you as my number two," Tony chuckled, as Phoenix looked relieved. "You'll just be one of the young guns I know who also deserves this great opportunity, if you will. To be honest, it'll probably be more of a sideways move. Yes, noses would be put out of joint, probably more so than if you just got a job there yourself. But in truth, I think New York would be a better fit for you. There's a lot more you can learn especially if you're dealing with companies on both sides of the Atlantic. The fact you've got experience in the European market will help your American clients and vice-versa."

"So you don't think I'm ready to run Guardian?" he said, thoughtful.

"Oh, I have no doubt you can do it since it is only a small boutique company. *However*, it's also a lot more paperwork and less hands on. At this stage of your career, I'm guessing you aren't as keen on the paperwork. Besides, it can only better your future the more experience you have before you become a boring manager," Tony teased.

"You're right, I do need some time to think this all over," he said.

"Talk to Boston and Jason. They'll help you make the right decision," Tony said.

That was exactly what Phoenix did and before he realised it, he was winging his way to New York to start his new job.

Chapter Two

It was ironic really, just when Phoenix finally thought the Chan brothers would be living together again, Boston went and decided he and Alyssa were moving to England. One to get away from Alyssa's very meddling but lovable rogue, Uncle Jack, and two, thanks to their brother-in-law, Jason's former sworn enemy turned pseudo cousin, Kai Kwong Lee, they had managed to get Alyssa's father, Frankie a triad boss out of Asia by faking his death. Boston thought England would be a better place to start fresh where Alyssa's father could masquerade as a relative they generously decided to let live with them. Only a very select few knew the real truth about Frankie's connection to them.

Years ago Boston had left his London apartment for Phoenix and now, left his New York one for his brother, along with the name of a friend's cousin to help show him around the town.

As Tony predicted, at first working in New York wasn't the most pleasant of times for Phoenix. Gossip was spread that some new senior executive had bought over some guy from England with him. Thus some of the employees in the Aurora Financial Services investment division were unhappy and snide comments made. Nevertheless, Phoenix trusted Tony's wisdom in this move and decided he wasn't going to care. If worst came to worst, he'd resign and go work somewhere else or even return to London. Besides, he also knew he would always have not only Tony's support, but his family's.

As it was, Phoenix's new team leader, Jon Johnson or JJ as he was known, was downright furious he was landed with this person he had no time for or wanted on his team. His team were slick talking go-getters who could sell a cemetery to a dead person or at least get the dead person to invest in it.

Now he was supposed to babysit some prissy English boy who was clearly the lover of some new senior executive.

"Look, Felix, I'll be honest. I don't want or need you in my team. I know you're only here because your lover boy wasn't planning on leaving you behind. So let's cut to the chase. Stay out of my way, don't bother me and we'll get along just fine," JJ said, upon meeting Phoenix.

Phoenix sat there stunned, unable to believe what he just heard. First the man was not only openly rude, but he just cast false aspersions on his and Tony's sexuality. JJ was worse than any manager or even jerk he had ever met.

"First of all, my name is *Phoenix* or if that's too hard for your little peabrain to remember, Nix is fine. Secondly, and most *importantly*, I'm not gay. Tony's not gay. He has a loving wife and family, and if I hear one word of you spreading that kind of slander around, I'll not only sue you for defamation, but I'll also kick your arse while I'm at it. Are we clear?" he said, trying to keep a lid on his rapidly rising temper.

JJ wasn't scared of this interloper trying to threaten him. He was the king around here. He rose, leaning on his desk eyeballing Phoenix.

"Just so *you know*, one tiny little mistake and your arse is fired. Am *I* clear?" JJ said.

Phoenix left JJ's office knowing he was going to kick the bastard in the balls when the time was right. With JJ's threats Phoenix now knew he needed to quickly get up to speed on the way things were done in America.

In the first few weeks, Phoenix couldn't understand why his clients were just two-bit mom and pop investors whereas in London they were multi-million dollar clients. Then he realised this was not only JJ's way of trying to break him, but this division in America was nowhere near as big as his old company in terms of money. Overall, Aurora was only a small player in the investment finance field and therefore Phoenix had more experience than JJ thought.

Luckily for Phoenix, once he cottoned onto JJ's tricks, he decided this was the perfect way to learn how Americans liked to invest.

"How's your first few weeks going?" Tony said, as they caught up one night over dinner.

Phoenix didn't have the heart to tell Tony the truth, that people were discussing not only their sexuality, but he and JJ had openly declared war.

"Interesting and different," he said.

"Got any good accounts yet?" Tony said.

"Just some small fry stuff at the moment, I'm sure they just want to let me get my feet wet before I handle any bigger accounts," he lied.

Sensing Phoenix wasn't telling him the truth, he left it, but even he'd heard rumblings about JJ and knew bringing Phoenix to New York with him wasn't the best idea. Perhaps he should have just waited and then poached Phoenix from Guardian at a later date, but he wanted to make it a clean break for them both at the same time. Tony truly thought that one day Phoenix would be either taking his job when he retired, or starting his own company and he wanted Phoenix to be prepared for either. Phoenix's genius could make the investment division of Aurora one of the best in the world.

"Want me to talk to JJ?" he said, making the offer just to reassure Phoenix he had his back if he needed it.

"No. I'll deal with him," Phoenix said. "What I do want to know is how investment finance works in America."

They spent the night discussing what they called 'the American way' and the following week, Phoenix spent so much time out of the office, JJ happily thought he was out looking for another job, but no such luck.

One month later, Phoenix's phone was constantly running hot and even his secretary Margaret struggled to keep up. JJ constantly snooped to see just what Phoenix was up to since he still made no moves to resign, but could never quite manage to piece anything together.

At the team meeting for the half yearly results, when every team leader and manager in the department were in attendance, JJ was annoyed to see Phoenix there.

"You don't belong here, this is for team *leaders* and higher ups, that's not you," he hissed.

Phoenix just smiled and took a seat. JJ wasn't sure if he should kick Phoenix out or tell someone else about him and let them do it. Instead he sat and tried hard to ignore the sliver of anxiety now snaking down his spine. He was missing something, but wasn't sure what it was and that's what had him worried.

"As you all know I'm retiring as director at the end of the week and Tony will be taking over from me," Bob Simmons said, motioning to Tony Santamaria.

Tony had spent his time while Bob was still the director getting up to speed on the systems and roles of everyone in the division to make the transition seamless.

"For many years JJ's team has been the highest investing team we have," Bob said.

JJ tried to look humble and modest, but couldn't hide his smirk.

"Well, now I am absolutely delighted to say the latest half yearly figures show we not only have a new winning team, but they dwarf everyone's numbers including JJ's in total. Not to mention it was also done in such a short amount of time," Bob said.

Seeing the admiration on Bob's face was more than JJ

could stand and he furiously stood, looking around.

"Who? Who's supposedly beaten my winning team? None of you here have ever been in touching distance, so for you to think you could surpass my team is impossible. Someone's putting up false figures," JJ said.

"Actually it was Phoenix's team," Bob said, now looking slightly uncomfortable by JJ's outburst.

"He doesn't have a team. He's part of mine. So there you go, I still win," JJ sniped.

"Actually, he's been his own team since he started," Nelson Fisher, the division manager and their immediate boss said. "Phoenix came to me and explained how it would be unfair to your team to have to accept a new person when you didn't need one. He asked for a chance to prove he could make it in America, without putting anyone out and I think the results show he's done that and more. Congratulations Phoenix."

Phoenix sat there trying his damnedest not to smirk or look too smug. He knew JJ was not only fuming about being bested, but trying to think of all the ways he could get payback.

After the meeting, JJ not unexpectedly, cornered Phoenix in the elevator.

"You bastard, you think you've won. You haven't won, I'm king here and you'll soon be on your way. I don't know how you managed to fake those numbers, but it won't last," he spat.

"If I were you, I'd think about getting a new job. It's clear to me you won't be happy in my shadow and I'm not going anywhere," Phoenix said. "Oh and by the way, I owe you something."

JJ wasn't sure what Phoenix was talking about, but as the elevator dinged and the doors began to open, Phoenix's fist crashed into JJ's face sending him reeling.

Phoenix strolled out of the elevator smiling, glad there was no one waiting to get in it as JJ was sprawled on the ground with a bloody nose. Serves him right, he thought.

Tony was having dinner with Phoenix when he brought up some news of interest.

"I told you, you could do it and even I have to say I'm more than impressed you not only put JJ's results to shame, but single-handedly almost doubled the department's revenue and in such a short amount of time. I also heard JJ had the most unfortunate accident, slipping and falling, bloodying his nose," Tony grinned.

"The first part is true, the second, I wouldn't know, but he deserved it," he smiled.

"That he did and I'm glad you managed to put him in his place. I'm sure he's now angrier than a disturbed wasps' nest," Tony said.

"That he is," he said.

"So how did you do it?" Tony said, intrigued.

"Do what?" He feigned ignorance until he knew exactly what Tony was asking.

"How did you end up beating him in the results and how did you bloody his nose?" Tony said.

"I believe a fist to the face got the job done, and I worked my arse off finding investors and investments which made great sense," he smiled. "What JJ doesn't realise is that in America some of what he considers small-fry investors actually have a lot of money. Sure it's a pittance to what I'm used to dealing with, but I managed to get them to agree to put them into a group together to get their money to go further."

Tony smiled at Phoenix's tactic. It was a great one.

"Also, some of those so-called small-fry, actually know a lot of wealthy people to whom they would then recommend me. I have to admit it was quite frightening when one man in his seventies went into his room and then came out with a large bag full of cash. I didn't know if he had robbed a bank or where you could hide such an amount." He laughed at the memory of Mr Schultz that day.

"So you weren't tempted to rob him yourself?" Tony laughed.

"It would have been so easy, but I couldn't do it," he said, shaking his head. "He told me that he didn't trust banks and no one, not even his children knew just how much money he had hidden."

"So what did you do with the money?" Tony said.

"Although he didn't want to do it, I had to explain that one, our company won't handle that much cash and two, these days everything is done electronically. You should have seen how paranoid I was when I escorted him to the bank. I was terrified someone would mug us the entire way," he said.

"So he's now got himself a bank account?" Tony said.

"Oh, he already had one. The cash was more of a rainy

day, just in case the end of the world came, type thing. But this will make you laugh. After I told him we really needed to put the money in the bank, he looked so forlorn that he took some back out and hid it," Phoenix chuckled.

"Did you see where and how much?" Tony grinned.

"Let's just say it was enough to buy a brand new, luxury, tailored just for you sports car," he said.

"Where does this client live again?" Tony teased.

Phoenix just tapped the side of his nose and smiled.

"Fine," Tony sighed. "Now back to JJ, no more of the former and a whole lot more of the latter, if you please."

"No problem but I warn you, JJ's not going to go down without a fight. He's been the undisputed king for so long that you'll probably hear a lot more gossip and rumours before I stomp him into the ground and claim my victory," he grinned, making Tony laugh once more.

After hearing about Phoenix's results the whole department was now abuzz in awe and looking at him in a new light. Forgotten were the snide comments and thoughts they previously had of him.

Phoenix's success escalated the war and JJ was determined to win. At every chance he got, JJ tried to either steal Phoenix's clients and leads, or just tried in general to make Phoenix look bad to anyone he could. He also unashamedly snooped to try and get whatever dirt he could to hopefully blackmail Phoenix with it.

As it happened, he only became even more enraged every time one of Phoenix's clients would just reconfirm their loyalty to him. JJ was the king of selling pipe dreams and snake oil, but for some reason none of Phoenix's clients ever bought anything that came out of his mouth. It took him a while to realise every time he went to try and poach one of Phoenix's clients, they would in turn tell Phoenix, which was why Phoenix always looked so smug.

Due to JJ's obsession with Phoenix, he not only let his own clients fall by the wayside, but he realised too late his own team had turned their backs on him and gone over to the enemy.

"Why the hell would you be talking to that dickhead? You know he's just going to eat you up and spit you out, *and* take all your clients and toss you aside," JJ roared, at poor Mitch, who he considered the weakest member of his team.

"Actually JJ, he's helped me to double my numbers and get a lot more clients, something you've never done for me," Mitch said, his voice full of disdain.

"What a load of crap. I bought you in and made you a member of a winning team," JJ scowled.

"No, what you did was give me all the crap clients you didn't want to have to deal with because they weren't making enough money for you. Every client I had that was worth something, you took for yourself. Nix is actually a team player, he wants us *all* to do well," Mitch said.

"You'll all regret this. He's doing a number on everyone and no one can see it and when he makes his move it'll be too late and you'll all regret not listening and sticking with me," he said.

"Sure, JJ, sure," Mitch said, walking away.

The next day, JJ resigned saying he found a better job

with a ton more money and prestige. No one even noticed he was no longer working there and Mitch got JJ's office.

From then on, employees just seemed to gravitate towards Phoenix. He tried hard to make time for everyone, but with his own workload it was hard to juggle. With an intuition even he couldn't understand, he just seemed to know which employees didn't have the skills for investment finance or should just remain assistants. Even though he was young and in some ways just as inexperienced as some of them, he still managed without even realising it, to change the department dynamics and working styles.

Tony called Phoenix into a meeting with Phoenix's boss, Nelson.

"Nix, I've been hearing some great things about you," Tony beamed. He was always happy when he could acknowledge Phoenix's genius out loud.

"Thanks," he said.

"Anyway, Nelson has been saying that since you've come on board, not only have all our results been skyrocketing, but the office is a completely different place," Tony said, knowing it was true as he had seen it with his own eyes.

The compliment made Phoenix redden.

"I don't think I can take the credit for that," he said.

"I've been watching you Nix, and you definitely can take all the credit. Since you've come on board, everyone gets along. There's no more infighting and I've seen the way everyone comes to you with their questions," Nelson smiled.

"That's great to hear, but I still think that you're blowing it out of proportion. I'm just doing my job and trying to help out the others," he said.

"And that's what makes you great management material," Nelson smiled.

"Huh?" he said, confused.

"We want to promote you to be my second in charge of the department," Nelson said, as Tony beamed.

"Second in charge?" Phoenix's eyes were wide as saucers. Never had he imagined being promoted so quickly. "B-but what about Walter?"

Nelson's face took to frowning his displeasure at the mention of his current number two.

"It seems Walter isn't happy with the office changes and has decided to move on," Nelson said.

Phoenix was now confused. Every time he talked to Walter he seemed happy enough. Clearly there was something else going on he didn't know about.

"When does Walter leave and when am I supposed to start?" he said.

"He's already left and you start tomorrow," Nelson said.

"T-tomorrow? So soon? Are you sure I'm the right person?" he said.

The attack of nerves hit Phoenix as Tony and Nelson just chuckled.

"You'll be fine as you'll just keep doing what you're doing along with more paperwork. Now I have to go and break the news to everyone in the department," Nelson said. "Congratulations Nix, you've truly earned it."

Phoenix sat there stunned and Tony beamed.

"I told you, didn't I, that you'd be shooting straight to the top and you're proving me right," he said.

"I still can't believe it," Phoenix said, shaking his head. "There are others who are infinitely more qualified than me."

"Yes, but as Nelson said, you changed the entire culture of the department. There's no more rivalry or pettiness going on. People are happy to work together and the fact you are actually helping them, shows you are a manager," Tony chuckled. "Hm, I believe I said words to the same effect to you once before and you didn't believe them then either."

"It was easy once JJ and then a couple of others left, they were quite toxic. Although I'm still in shock about Walter," he said, still in disbelief that Nelson's number two resigned.

"Speaking of which, now this is just between you and me, but Walter was cut from the same cloth as JJ and wasn't exactly management material. He was only tolerated since there never seemed to be anyone else able to take over. However, from the time I've been watching from afar and Nelson's honest observations, it seemed anyone worthy of replacing Walter always seemed to resign to move onto greener pastures, if you will. Thanks to you, Nelson now had a good reason to let Walter go," Tony said.

Phoenix was stunned by the implication that Walter hadn't just willingly resigned, but was pushed out the door because of him and he felt a little guilty over it.

Seeing Phoenix's face, Tony went to reassure him.

"Don't feel guilty. Like I said, when I saw how the department was running, I could tell that Walter wasn't a good fit and needed to find the right time to dismiss him. It was always going to happen," Tony said.

Phoenix got the hint. It seemed Walter was indeed the same as JJ, not that he had much to do with Walter as he mainly dealt with Nelson. Now he was thankful for it because if Walter knew what Phoenix was doing, he was sure JJ would have found out much earlier. Their war would have been not only messier, but JJ may have actually won.

"And in regards to JJ, he was fired from his new job after a week and is now trying to peddle himself with his own company. I'm telling you, I wouldn't be surprised if he ends up running some kind of Ponzi scheme," Tony said.

"Fired? Really?" Phoenix rubbed his chin. "You're probably right, JJ is the kind of slick snake oil salesman who will happily take everyone's money and give nothing in return."

After Phoenix told Boston and Jason about his promotion, they both came over to New York to celebrate with him. Phoenix was embarrassed by the fuss, yet appreciated the support.

The three of them and Tony, all went out to celebrate, noting this was just the first small step on Phoenix's upward trajectory to success. Then they took bets on when Phoenix would be running the department or even the whole of Aurora, they had that much faith in him.

Now as Phoenix continued to look out his office window, he scrubbed his face with his hands knowing something needed to change. How depressing and grown-up it was, he thought before sitting back down at his desk and continuing to work into the early hours of the morning.

Tony was right on the money. Being a manager meant a lot more paperwork and reports, but still he retained some of his favourite clients like the Nix Six as he called them. The six little mom and pop investors who he not only made wealthier thanks to their trust in him, but were the ones who helped send him on his way and with their loyalty also helped to take down JJ.

It was JJ's short-sightedness and his Achilles heel at only seeing what the client was worth on paper. He only wanted the biggest and wealthiest clients. Whereas Phoenix's thinking outside the box to include groups of friends or those with the same financial goals together meant he could help everyone, big or small.

It also gave people a chance to get to know the way he operated and in gaining their trust meant they would in turn spread the word that Phoenix Chan would not only be honest in his dealings, but could help you with any amount of investment.

While it might not be big or flashy, he brought something even more priceless. Loyalty.

Chapter Three

Jacqueline Richmond considered herself to be a worldly woman after living in New York most of her life. She also wasn't conceited enough to think herself stunning, with her dark brown hair and hazel eyes, which wasn't exactly unique in the metropolitan city. However, she did have an extremely well-paying job, thanks to not only working in the family business, but also being her brother's executive assistant. The only downside was she did *all* the work while Charles took *all* the credit and glory.

She could even say she was in the prime of her life: healthy, owned her own apartment, dated and had various boyfriends. The flipside was all her boyfriends were always very fleeting or more to the point, she just didn't seem to know how to pick a good man. This is what brought her to one of her favourite places in the world, Finnigan's Finest Meats.

She called over the counter to the older man wearing the butcher's apron.

"Hey, Alf," she said.

"Hi Jacs. What'll it be today? I've got some delicious eye filet," he said.

"No thanks. I'm in the mood to pound the crap out of something," she said.

"Uh-oh. Which boyfriend are we up to again?" Alf chuckled, yet there was concern in his eyes.

There was no doubting Jacqui was pretty, but unfortunately Alf, who had known her from when she was young, also knew Jacqui had the worst luck with men starting with her chauvinist father and stupid, lazy brother.

"The drug dealer," she said, depressed.

"Drug dealer?" he said, stunned and confused. "I thought it was the accountant or was it the shop guy?"

"No, they were ages ago. Keep up, Alf. Keep up," she smiled, enjoying teasing the older man.

Alfred Finnigan was in his sixties, she thought, with greying hair and warm brown eyes that crinkled every time he smiled. He and Gene Richmond were friends from back in the day when they both lived in the same neighbourhood, with Alf also becoming one of Gene's first clients when Gene started Aurora Financial Services, and thus Alf knew the Richmond family very well.

To Jacqui, Alf was the only father figure she knew who seemed to actually care about her life, and who also happened to give great advice.

Jacqui's own father had never taken much interest in her,

not even to placate her when she was ranting about some injustice she or the world was suffering, or even when she succeeded or was happy. In Gene Richmond's mind, his daughter, like all women, was inconsequential to his life. When he was married to his first wife, Jacqui's mother, Fleur he also hadn't cared to actually listen to his wife's opinions. They didn't matter. They didn't count. To Gene, it was a man's world and that was all that mattered. Now he was currently in the midst of divorcing wife number two and still he thought his way was the right way.

"Sorry," Alf grinned. "The trouble with you modern women, you're too busy dating and dropping men like you try on shoes. You need to be fussier, hold out a while longer and get the pair you really like *and* that fits perfectly."

"I'll remember that the next time I date someone. Although I don't know if a guy would really be into hearing 'you're not the right shoe. I'm looking for comfy slippers'," she giggled.

"You *know* what I mean." He scowled in his normal friendly manner, handing her a brown paper wrapped parcel. "Here, have some chuck steak. Give it a good beating, but for tonight, eat the eye filet."

"Thanks, Alf. If only you were thirty or so years younger," she sighed.

"You know it. I'd give all your young bucks a good run for their money," he smiled.

She waved and left the butchery with the doorbell chiming on her way out.

Alf was right about one thing, Jacqui thought. She

shouldn't have just jumped in and started dating Allen. Admittedly, he seemed like any other normal guy at first and she hadn't noticed any obvious connections to the seedy underworld, not that there should be any reason why she would even be suspicious or looking.

It wasn't until Allen began to start getting newer things with more frequency: a car, clothes and even a fancy Rolex, which started making Jacqui suspicious. How could a man who only earned an average wage suddenly become so flush with money? Yet, never once had she asked where or how he got all this stuff.

The only reason she and Allen broke up was because he traded Jacqui in for a clichéd blonde before he got caught by the cops for dealing in drugs.

Although Jacqui was thankful for her lucky escape, having the police turn up on her doorstep with routine questions about Allen, and her being unable to provide many answers, left her feeling stupid, but also mad at herself she hadn't seen it at all. If she had, she would have been very tempted to turn Allen into the police herself or at least left an anonymous tip. This was why she was now currently punishingly tenderising a poor innocent piece of steak. She was just trying to work through her man issues and boy, did she have plenty.

She just might have to take Alf's advice. No more just dating because she was asked out. Instead she was going to try waiting to see if she could get herself a better pair of shoes. Maybe next time, she'd make sure that they were comfortable ones like slippers, and not, make your legs look long and slender, sexy ones.

Yes, no more sexy shoes for her. Practical shoes only.

Jacqui worked at Aurora Financial Services, a company her father started and built into a multi-million dollar empire, and although she might work for her brother, Charles as his executive assistant, the big corner office with the shiny brass plate on the door should have her name on it, not his.

"Jacs, can you come in here, please?" Charles said.

Charles Richmond was not only her younger brother, but had also been the owner of Aurora for the past few years when their father just handed it over to him on a silver platter. An act which not only shocked both Charles and Jacqui, but also made her furious.

Charles was an idiot who couldn't add his way out of a paper bag, let alone manage any of the complex accounts their clients had. He also didn't have a head for business management.

It was Jacqui who had always done Charles' homework and got him A's. Of course if she knew then what she knew now, she never would have done it. But at the time she thought she was saving her brother from the guilt of disappointment from their father. Gene Richmond had not only expected Charles to follow him into the family firm, but to eventually take it over when he decided to retire. Of course when Gene was ecstatic by Charles' grades, Jacqui basked in the reflective praise.

However, the one thing their parents couldn't understand

was how Charles could get A's in class, but only just manage to pass an exam. Somehow to Jacqui's disbelief, Charles managed to get their parents to believe that he was just poor at taking exams.

Jacqui on the other hand, couldn't believe her parents bought that boloney and yet, wasn't surprised since it did seem to make sense. If she had been smarter, she would have made his homework less stellar.

"What's up, Charles?" she said, entering his office and sitting down.

"I wanted you to be the first to officially know the company is looking for a buyer," he said.

"You're selling dad's company?" she said, shocked.

While Charles had casually mentioned the possibility before, she never thought he would actually do it. Aurora was their family legacy. It had a good reputation in the corporate world and now Charles just wanted to sell it? Their father was going to go ballistic.

"It's *my* company, Jacs, so I can do whatever I want with it," he said, petulant.

"But it's *our* legacy," she said.

"No, it's a millstone hanging around my neck. You know how much I *hate* this place," he said.

"Then let me have it. I'll run it," she said.

She knew she sounded desperate and his laughter just confirmed that.

"Are you kidding? Dad would have a fit and not only that, I'd have no money," he said.

"I'd share the profits with you," she said, in earnest.

"Sorry Jacs, it's never going to happen. I'm selling," he said.

She knew that stubborn tone. It was the same tone their father used in his stupid, *I'm a man so I know best* or *it makes no difference what you think, I'm right*. It was a tone which had grated on her all her life.

While it wasn't nice to think ill of your own parents, this time was different. Gene was foolish for marrying the conniving, mercenary soon to be ex-wife number two, Majorie who was trying to get around their pre-nup and take him to the cleaners. He was also idiotic for retiring and leaving Charles to run the company, thinking it would then mean he would have less alimony to pay, when Jacqui was a better choice.

That's what made Jacqui angry the most at their father and more so, Charles. She was the smart one in the family and that wasn't even being conceited. It was the truth.

No, her father was a stupid male chauvinist. Stupid to still think men were better than women in this day and age.

Now Charles was announcing he was planning on selling their family business. Just like that. No questions. No consideration for her. Nothing. Her brother was stupid! Stupid! Stupid!

Charles had gone straight to work at Aurora after high school instead of going to university and getting an accounting degree, somehow persuading their father this way was more beneficial. At the time, Jacqui was astonished by the move even though she knew Charles probably couldn't have gained his degree without any subterfuge.

Remembering when she finished university and Charles claimed he needed her to be his assistant, begging her to come and work for him in the family business. He would teach her the ropes for good wages and she could also study to become a registered accountant at the same time.

At the time Jacqui honestly thought Charles was being kind and wanted a closer relationship. When she thought back on her naïveté as Charles had only wanted her as his assistant because he couldn't do anything required of him, she wanted to kick herself at how she had entrapped herself in this deceit. It amazed her how Charles had gotten away with it for so long. Surely someone, even their father, must have realised he was hopeless. Now it was too late and she had become his glorified work slave.

She should have left and let the truth be shone on Charles, but she didn't want to let their father down or even humiliate Charles, after all, he was still her brother. However, when Charles' standard of work dramatically improved, he took all the glory and basked in it.

How many times had she heard their father say, "All Charles needed was a bit of time to get settled." Did their father honestly believe what he was saying or was it more wanting to remain ignorant to the reality? Whichever it was, Jacqui was now doing everything for Charles. When he was promoted to director of Aurora's accountancy division, Charles insisted she stay with him and bribed her with a hefty pay rise. She even took his meetings for him and soon people just came to her for everything they needed with Aurora's clients thinking it was wonderful that brother and sister worked so closely together.

When Charles went on a six week holiday, no one even realised except their father, who told Jacqui that she was doing a good job. And, that's what really kept her slaving away. Her father's praise.

Now she wasn't even going to have the family business any more thanks to her stupid brother.

They say things happen in threes and therefore Jacqui must have done something to anger the gods because she had *four* horrible things happen to her. In an unbelievable twist of fate, she managed to have *two* fender benders in the same week.

In the first, she hit the car in front as she thought they were moving forward, only for them to suddenly stop and she kept going. In the second, someone hit her doing pretty much the same thing she had done only days earlier. Ironic? Yes!

And the third thing? Well, that was a blind date gone horrendously wrong.

Jacqui's old college friend, had a boyfriend whose friend, would be perfect for her.

"Don't worry, Theo and I will double date with you. I promise, Gavin is a great guy," Linda said.

It hadn't sounded too scary if Linda and Theo came along and so Jacqui agreed.

The only problem with the night in her opinion, was Gavin. Gavin was a loud, obnoxious, arrogant creep.

Dinner had been torturous with him not only talking over

everyone but also telling them, if they dared to disagree with him, they were wrong. He sneered and even condescended to Jacqui, making her realise he was also a male chauvinist. How could Linda have thought Gavin was a nice guy? To Jacqui's misery, all Gavin did was remind her of her own father the entire date.

"Jacs, I'm so sorry," Linda said, profusely apologetic when they went to freshen up. "I have no idea what happened to Gavin. All the times I've met him, he's been lovely."

"It's fine," she said, magnanimous. "After the week I've had, this is probably par for the course."

"Are you sure?" Linda said, hesitant.

"Sure. However, no more set-ups. Promise?" she said.

"Promise," Linda said.

They both looked relieved their friendship was still intact and Linda wasn't planning on meddling in Jacqui's love life anymore.

The fourth and probably worst thing to happen to her, something which still made her head spin, was Charles wanting to sell the company. There was no way she could let Charles sell the company without their father's knowledge and after she finally summoned up enough courage, she went to bravely tell him. She didn't care if it looked like she was ratting Charles out. She was!

"Dad, I think you should know Charles is thinking of selling the company," she said.

"What?" Gene roared. "Why on earth would he want to do that?"

"Because he doesn't want to run it anymore," she said.

"Well, that at least makes sense," he said.

"Dad, did you even hear what I just said? Charles wants to sell the company. The company you built from nothing. He wants to get rid of your *legacy*," she said.

"Well, if he doesn't want to run it, I guess it's better we get top dollar for it," he said.

Jacqui couldn't believe how nonchalant her father was acting. Like he thought Charles was doing the right thing.

"I'll run it. I do everything now anyway," she said.

This was her last chance to save not only the family business, but to get her father's agreement. Instead, he just laughed.

"You? You run the business? Oh honey, it's a lovely thought, but you wouldn't be able to handle the stress and make the big decisions required. You need to have strength and think like a man to get the deals done. Let's face it, women can't run a company like Aurora, we'd go under in a year," he chuckled. "Besides, as soon as you get married and have children, you'll no longer be interested in the company. It's not a toy, Jacqueline. It takes dedication and motivation to keep it going. You can't just do all the easy bits."

His scold not only humiliated her, but made her want to slap him silly while railing against his chauvinistic attitude. But since she had known him her entire life, she sighed resigned to the reality and kept her anger to herself.

"How's the divorce going?" she said.

The only reason Gene gave up running the company and handed it to Charles was to hopefully pay less alimony to the witch Marjorie, a woman he foolishly married on a whim because she flattered his ego, and then once the ring was on her finger made his life a misery. It was something which should have made Jacqui sad for her father, however she was terrible enough to be a bit schadenfreude over it. It made her feel like karma bit him on the bottom and yet, he didn't even see it.

"Typical woman. Throwing tantrums about money. How she needs more, that she can't manage on the pittance she's getting. She's dragged it out as long as she could and thankfully it's almost over now that she's finally realising I'm not willing to give her more than what was stated in the pre-nup. She's lucky to even be getting that considering she wasn't a faithful or great wife who kept my house clean and dinner on the table when I got home from work. Perhaps, if she had, I would have been more inclined to give her a few more dollars," Gene grumbled.

Gene and Marjorie's whole relationship just reinforced in his mind just how useless women were, which made Jacqui grit her teeth in frustration.

"So you're not going to stop Charles from selling the company?" She hadn't wanted to return to the topic, but needed to know if her father was even going to consider it.

"Honey, you need to find yourself a husband and have some children, then you won't even need to try and understand how the business world works. Charles is doing what he thinks is right for him. I'll chat to him about it, but I'm sure he's looked at all the angles properly. He wouldn't be my son, nor would I have given him the company if he wasn't as smart as a whip," he said.

Feeling her anger begin to boil once again, Jacqui slammed her father's front door on the way out, but all that did was make Gene sigh at how childish and emotional Jacqueline was. Yet another reason why she'd never make it any further than a secretary.

If last week was bad, this week started off even worse when Charles called Jacqui into his office.

"I can't believe you tattled on me to dad," he raged.

"I wanted to make sure he knew just what you were up to. This is *our* family business, Charles. *Our legacy*," she said, defiant.

"Well, thanks to you I got lectured and moaned at," he said, annoyed.

"So, what's the final decision?" she said, nervous.

"I agreed to stick it out for a year to just ensure I wasn't being rash," he moaned.

"That's great," she smiled.

When Charles told his wife, Cynthia what Jacqui had done and what his father said, she was understandably furious.

"I thought you wanted to give up that crappy job and for us to live how we dreamed in Europe doing all the wheeling and dealings with the big boys, and now you're telling me we're still tied to this horrible company for another year?" she shrieked.

The one thing Cynthia didn't realise was that Charles wasn't the businessman she thought she married. He never told his wife Jacqui did all the work and thus, all the money and profit they made, which wasn't to be sneezed at, was because of Jacqui's hard work, not his. Still, he didn't want the company, had never wanted the company. What he really wanted was the glamorous lifestyle of the rich and famous just like his wife.

"We'll secretly sell the business," she said.

"What?" he said, shocked.

"We'll secretly sell the business. No one needs to know. It's perfect. And by the time anyone finds out, it'll be too late," she smiled.

"Jacs will know. People will want to see the company's financials and all that, Cynthia," he said.

"Well, just give them old stuff or something. Surely you can work around it, can't you, darling? I mean, this is our future. We're meant to live our lives with the rich and fabulous. Sailing on our superyacht in the Mediterranean in the summer, sipping champagne and eating caviar while wearing only the top designers," she said, running her finger down his chest. "Don't you want to see me in skimpy little bikinis all day, or running around topless, as the Europeans do?"

Charles was getting aroused and knew that's exactly what he wanted.

"You know I do," he rasped, starting to remove his clothes.

"Then don't you think you owe it to us to get this show on the road. After all, we're in the prime of our lives, we don't want to be old and grey," she said.

Afterwards, Cynthia knew Charles would do as she suggested and find a buyer he could secretly sell too. After all, he not only wanted to keep her happy, but he didn't want to be stuck with a company he hated any more than she did.

"Hi Alf," Jacqui said, entering the butchery.

"Hi, Jacs. What'll it be today?" He hadn't seen her in a few weeks.

"What do you have to get over a bad few weeks?" she said.

"I've got just the thing. How about either some gourmet sausages, venison, chicken or a rack of lamb?" he said.

"Hm, it all sounds good. Maybe I should go with the chicken and then I can have chocolate pudding for dessert as well to make up for it," she said.

"Uh-oh. Who's the guy this time?" Alf said, concerned. "I thought we agreed you'd be more patient and not just jump into another relationship. You can't have dated and dumped some loser so quickly, can you? That's got to be a record even for you."

"Ouch that hurts, Alf. Where's the faith? But no, no guy this time, sort of. Would you believe it was two fender benders, one which wasn't my fault," she hastily said, after seeing Alf's dismay. "And I have been taking your advice."

He arched his eyebrows in curiosity.

"I've become fussier about my men just like you suggested. Although I also probably had the world's worst blind date *ever*, the other night for my troubles," she said.

"Well, since you're doing blind dates and all, I happen to know a guy," he smiled.

Jacqui wasn't too sure about another blind date, yet didn't want to offend her friend.

"My age and single?" she said, sceptical.

"Of course, I'm married remember," he laughed.

"You might be, but I bet you have lots of *old* buddies that are single, right?" she said.

"You got me there, but it's definitely none of them. Although, they would all owe me big time if I set them up on a date with you," he grinned. "Come on Jacs, would *I* do that to you?"

She rolled her eyes at Alf's attempt to sound mortally wounded by her accusation.

"Probably not, but after the other night, I don't want to be sitting there thinking that getting a root canal is better," she said, making them both chuckle.

"No, he's a good guy. You'd like him. Handsome, *young*, good manners, funny," he said, extolling her future blind date's virtues.

"Does Mr Perfect have a name?" she said.

"Edward. How are you for next Friday night, dinner at Kanda?" he said.

"Great, if you're paying," she teased, and then sighed. "Fine. It really can't be any worse than any of the men I've picked out myself. Just don't blame me if it all goes pear shaped. Call me to confirm the time."

Alf beamed as Jacqui exited the shop shaking her head unable to believe she had now just agreed to a blind date set up by her butcher of all people.

The only logical reason Jacqui could come up with as to why she agreed at all, was because Alf had not only caught her at a weak moment, but he probably did know a nice guy that just might suit her.

As it turned out, she returned to Alf's the next day to get some gourmet sausages and he confirmed her blind date then.

"I talked to Edward. He said he'll met you at seven at Kanda on Friday night. I'm paying so don't worry and he'll be holding a yellow rose for you," he said, pleased with himself.

"Wow, talk about striking while the iron's hot," she said, surprised by the speed of it all. "You do realise that if this doesn't work out, you can't blame me when I find a new butcher."

"It'll be great and if nothing else, you'll have a nice meal on me," he said.

"I'm warning you. One chauvinistic, patronising, condescending remark or put-down and I'm out of there," she said, half teasing and a little serious.

"Doesn't bother me. It's not *my* date," he grinned.

"Then I'm going to order the most expensive things on the menu whether I like it or not. That'll serve you right," she laughed. "Just who is this Edward guy to you anyway?"

"A friend's son. Colin's wife has been on at him about why Edward never seems to date nice girls."

Jacqui groaned at Alf's words. No one wanted to be considered as the *nice* girl, even if they were.

"Thanks for the sausages. I'll let you know how it goes," she said, waving on her way out of the shop.

Chapter Four

So this is what it had come down to, Jacqui sighed to herself. Her dating life had flat-lined so badly she was now going on a blind date set up by her butcher.

There was no harm in going because like she told Alf, it couldn't be any worse than the dates she picked for herself. Although it would probably take a minor miracle to make tonight a great date, she'd be completely happy to call it a success if it wasn't too awkward.

After purposely arriving at the restaurant ten minutes late just to be sure Edward would be there before her, Jacqui entered Kanda relieved the place was busy. Looking around for a man with a yellow rose, she couldn't see anyone who fit the description. Damn, so much for that tactic to help ease her nerves. She hoped he hadn't either thought to do the same thing or even worse, was standing her up.

"Excuse me," she said, to the maître d'. "I'm wondering

if you have a reservation for an Edward, Jacqui or Alf? Or have you seen a man holding a yellow rose?"

She had to give the maître d' his due because he didn't even raise an eyebrow at her questions, which made her wonder if this type of thing happened a lot here. However, the somewhat sympathetic or pitying look he gave her made her redden.

"Sorry madame, but there has been no one who has arrived with a rose of any colour at all," he said, with a rueful shake of his head. "However, there is a reservation for Jacqueline and Edward. Would you like me to show you to your table?"

Unsure what to do, her choices were to either go and sit at the table alone or go to the bar and order a drink.

"Do you mind if I just go to the bar and have a drink and wait?" she said, hoping this was the less embarrassing option if he had already seen her and left, or she had simply been stood up.

"Not at all. Just let me know when you are ready to be seated," he said.

At least the maître d'was too polite to say, *if you want to be seated at all, depending on whether your date turns up or not*.

Nervously she went to the bar and jiggled on the stool as she sat and sipped her drink, looking at her watch. She'd give him another ten minutes and if he hadn't turned up by then, she was leaving. There was no way she was eating here alone, that was one embarrassment she didn't need.

A pair of caramel eyes followed the striking woman as

she walked over to the bar and sat. Wanting to see what his blind date looked like before committing himself to a dinner, which could be an awkwardness he didn't need to subject himself to, he was happy to note she had a slender frame and the standard issue little black dress she was wearing was classy. She didn't seem to scream desperate at all.

Although it sounded shallow and superficial, he didn't care. What he did want to know was why someone was desperate enough to agree to a blind date? What was wrong with her? After talking to the maître d' who pointed in her direction, he knew for certain this woman was supposed to be Eddie's date tonight.

How Phoenix got himself into these situations he didn't know. Actually he did know. Eddie was supposed to be here, but instead found himself with a family emergency and gave Phoenix an urgent call to give his blind date the message because he didn't have the woman's number to tell her he couldn't make it.

What made this message even more important was that it wasn't just a blind date Eddie was supposed to be going on. It was also a favour for his dad's friend because the friend knew someone who could use better taste in men.

Phoenix shook his head in disbelief all the while thinking this whole thing seemed ludicrous to him.

Looking at the woman who was to be Eddie's date, there was nothing he could glean from first appearances. He noticed a few men at the bar appreciatively glancing at her, yet she was oblivious to it. He unkindly let her finish half her drink before making his move, but before he could even take two steps, another man who had been at the bar walked over to her and she smiled at him.

Phoenix froze waiting to see what she would do and felt himself exhale a breath when he saw her brushing the other man off. Points for that, he thought. She would be well within her rights to have gone off with the stranger since technically Edward hadn't shown up.

As she turned to finish her drink, he came up behind her and spoke.

"Jacqueline?" he said, trying to sound hesitant, yet he was very certain and as she swivelled in the stool to face him, he received the sunniest smile he had ever seen. She was radiant up close with that smile and he felt his body ratchet up a notch.

"Edward?" she said, nervous.

"Actually, Eddie couldn't make it, that's why I'm late," he said.

Her face went from bright to deflated as a flicker of disappointment crossed it.

"Don't worry about it," she said. "No harm done. Thank you for telling me."

Her words may have been polite, but he knew she was trying hard not to show how annoyed and disappointed she was. She slid off the stool and went to leave, but he blocked her way.

"Wait. Don't go," he said.

Real smooth, Phoenix inwardly groaned to himself, but he had her attention as those beautiful hazel eyes looked at him.

"Have dinner with me instead. That's why I'm here. Eddie asked me to take his place so you'd at least get dinner," he lied.

Jacqui hesitated. It was a nice offer, but she wasn't anyone's charity case. Mind you, Alf was paying the bill and this was a nice restaurant. *And* it would be better than feeling like this night was a complete failure.

"*Please*," he said, now feeling guilty for putting her in an awkward position.

His voice made her shiver and she noted his chiselled and strong face with eyes which made her think of decadent caramel fudge.

Knowing she should just leave, yet she was here now and hearing her stomach loudly rumbling, it would have been childish and immature to give up a free dinner.

"And just what lame excuse does Edward have for ditching me?" she said, unable to hide her annoyance at the thought this was some kind of terrible joke being played on her.

"He had a family emergency," he said, and even though she hadn't done it, Phoenix could tell she was rolling her eyes and snorting with disbelief to herself.

"*Please,* not that old chestnut. Do I look like I was born yesterday?" she said.

"It's true. He would have called you himself, but he didn't know your number. His sister was giving birth to her first child and there's been some serious complications. The whole family have rushed to the hospital to be there," he said.

Jacqui now felt not only very embarrassed, but contrite and guilty.

"I'm sorry for being so rude to you," she said.

"Don't worry about it. I'm sure your nerves were wound so tight waiting for Eddie. Not to mention you've probably already driven yourself to the brink of insanity just in the lead up to tonight's blind date as you wondered why Eddie needed to be set up. What was wrong with him? Did he have some sort of defective personality, which is why he needed to be set up?" he said. "Along with you then thinking that maybe he was thinking those same thoughts about you. It's probably driven you crazy."

"Who are you? Some sort of psychologist?" she said.

He chuckled and she felt the vibrations making her toes curl. If she couldn't have Edward, this guy seemed to be the next best thing.

"I'm not a therapist of any kind. I just used plain old logic. Doesn't everyone think like that before a blind date? Drive themselves mad going round and round thinking about what is wrong with the other person or whether that person might be thinking the exact same things about them?" he said.

"So what's wrong with you that you're here with me on a Saturday night and not out with your girlfriend?" she said, intrigued.

"It just so happens I'm between women at the moment," he grinned. "And even if I did have one, I still would have come by to let you know about Eddie."

His answer mollified her a little.

"Right. So what's your longest relationship with a

woman? When was your last girlfriend? Did you dump her or she dump you and why?" she said.

"Wow, talk about not beating around the bush. Would you have asked Eddie all these direct questions?" he said.

"Probably, but in a more subtle way," she grinned.

Jacqui had no idea why she was acting so passive-aggressive with this man. It wasn't like it was his fault he was sitting opposite her for dinner.

"Let's see, my longest relationship with a woman has to be my mother and no, we haven't dumped each other yet. Although I'm sure she has silently disowned me a few times while I was growing up," he said.

"You know I didn't mean with your family," she smiled.

"Oh, well next time you should be a bit more specific," he grinned, and she couldn't help but laugh. "Longest relationship was probably a couple of years when I was a lot younger and at university. Last girlfriend was six months ago and she dumped me for being a workaholic. You?"

"So you're a workaholic?" she said.

"Yes and no. I've been so busy trying to climb the corporate ladder I don't have much time to put into a relationship, thus all the women dump me. I'm not a complete workaholic, just ninety percent of the time. Your turn," he said, making sure she knew he wasn't about to let her off the hook that easily. "Why are you still single?"

Jacqui gave a heavy sigh. Five simple words. A common enough question, but did she dare tell him the truth that she was incapable of finding a great guy, or did she give him the very heavily diluted version. She looked at him and decided since he told her the truth, the least she could do was return the favour.

It seemed almost liberating she could be completely honest with him because he wasn't expecting anything from her tonight.

"The truth is, I'm a terrible judge of men," she said, and saw him give that smile which said he didn't believe her. "I'm serious. My last boyfriend turned out to be a drug dealer. Luckily he had already dumped me before he was arrested and I found out the truth." She couldn't help but smile at his look of surprise. "Then my friend recently set me up on a blind date with her, her boyfriend and his friend. The friend turned out to be the most chauvinistic, opinionated, horrible guy. My friend apologised saying she had never seen my date act like such a jerk before. There was also an accountant I went out with who turned out to be two-timing his girlfriend with me, not to mention the wannabe gangbanger. The list goes on," she sighed.

Phoenix couldn't have been more surprised if he tried. It was nice Jacqui was being so truthful, but how did one woman seem to attract the wrong kind of men? He almost felt sorry for her.

Then she saw the look on her switched blind date's face.

"Don't you dare feel sorry for me," she scowled.

"I'm not," he lied. "I'm just a little surprised one person could have such bad luck, that's all."

"Liar," she said.

"Okay, you got me," he said. "But I really am surprised. I don't think I've ever heard of any woman having the luck with men you've had and I've got four sisters so I should know."

"Four sisters!" she gasped, her eyes boggling wide in disbelief. "Holy cow, that's a lot. I've only got a brother, but I used to wish all the time I had a sister. I bet it was chaos being outnumbered by girls. Are they older or younger?"

Phoenix smiled. Jacqueline's face filled with curiosity made her look beautiful. Her hazel eyes were bright and wide and her smile shone and lit up her face. He could tell she truly was interested and not just being polite.

"Actually there's six of us altogether —"

"Six! Your poor parents," she said.

"Hey, they're the ones who had us," he chuckled.

"Tell me more," she said, eager to hear.

She had never met anyone with so many siblings. It must have been wonderful growing up with them all. It was only her and Charles and although he wasn't the kind of brother she could depend upon or was that close to, she still loved him.

"I have two older sisters and then it's me and my older brother and then my two younger sisters," he said, knowing Jacqueline was going to be gobsmacked when he named them, most people were.

Over the years when the Chan siblings told anyone their names, the reactions varied from polite laughter, honest amusement and people giving them horrified looks of *what were your parents thinking*. Although some of them never used to, now all the siblings loved their names and it made for good ice-breakers or party games.

"Oh wow," she said, before realising she knew more about his family and yet, didn't even know his name. How embarrassing and rude. "I don't mean to be rude, but I've actually just realised I don't even know your name."

"Phoenix. And you're Jacqueline," he said.

"Jacqui or Jacs is fine. Jacqueline sounds so formal," she said. "I hope I don't sound even more rude, but you don't sound American. Are you English?"

Phoenix thought Jacqui looked lovely with flushed cheeks as she asked such inquisitive questions.

"Actually I'm from New Zealand and lived in London for a few years before moving to New York," he said.

"Oh, New Zealand. That's in Europe, isn't it?" she said.

He stifled his laughter. It wasn't new to find out people didn't know where New Zealand was.

"No," he said, as her face turned bright red in embarrassment. "It's actually in the Pacific Ocean down by Australia."

"Sorry, that was embarrassing," she said.

"Don't worry, I get it all the time," he said, trying to put her at ease.

"You do?" she said, amazed.

"You'd be surprised," he said.

The wink Phoenix gave her made her toes curl and her stomach flutter. This lovely handsome man with the very sexy accent wasn't what she pictured at all tonight and yet, she was glad to have met him.

"So your name's Phoenix?" she said, hesitant. "Did your parents name you after the city or the mythical bird?" She knew she was sounding very nosy, yet couldn't help but be curious about the man sitting opposite her. Something about him just made her want to know more.

"The city," he said. "They had a thing for American places. Bet you can't guess the names of my siblings."

"Oh, I don't think I could —"

"Two are named after States. Another two, State capitals and two are just plain old cities," he smiled.

"You're kidding," she said.

There was that cute wide-eyed surprised look on her face again. He was beginning to like that look.

"Well, I know I'll never get the names of the cities so I'll stick to the States. There's fifty States so you'll have to help give me some clues, okay?" She smiled at the thought that this was at least a safe topic and was also a little bit of fun. "I'm ruling out anything with a compass point in their names and Illinois. I can't imagine anyone calling their child, Illinois."

"I agree," he said, enjoying watching the woman opposite him work it out. She intrigued him, something which hadn't happened in a long time.

"California and anything with a 'land' on the end and 'New' at the beginning is also gone."

Again he nodded his agreement.

"I can't see why you'd call your child, Hawaii, Washington or Alaska either," she said, but then looked thoughtful. "Oh, I have heard people called Washington, so that's back on the list, and I guess you could call your child Alaska so I'll put that on my 'if I've run out of logical States' list, just in case."

Jacqui looked annoyed she was re-adding names and not deleting them, which made him grin. Phoenix couldn't imagine anyone in his family being called Alaska Chan. That sibling probably would have changed their name by now.

"Now it's getting harder because some States people might use as a name even if no one thinks that it's a name for a child, you know?" she said.

"Like Alaska?" he teased.

"Yes, like Alaska," she laughed.

While they ate their food she was deep in thought.

Maybe this wasn't such a great idea, he thought to himself as they sat in silence or with Jacqui talking rhetorically to herself.

"Why don't I —"

"Shh," she said, making him chuckle.

She was so engrossed in working it out that she didn't want any help or interruptions breaking her train of thought.

"I haven't said their names yet, right?" she said, suspiciously. Wondering if he'd somehow deceived her.

"No. I'd tell you if you've mentioned it, but you haven't," he said.

"I just can't see someone being called Pennsylvania or Louisiana, but it's not improbable especially if they shorten it to Penny or Louise. I think they'll have to go on my Alaska list," she said.

"True. However, I promise none of their names are like that," he said, in an effort to give her a clue.

"Okay, I need a *tiny* hint. Just a tiny one," she said,

making sure he knew that she wanted to get this on her own.

"Would you like to know the letters they start with or the amount of letters in each name? Or perhaps the region in America," he said.

"Oh, I like that. Give me the amount of letters," she said.

"My elder sisters both have seven letters in their names."

"Oh brother," she sighed. "That's really not helpful."

He almost laughed when he saw the lightbulb switch on in her head.

"I've got it. Georgia or Florida?" she said, excited.

She was so happy he almost didn't have the heart to have to tell her she was wrong.

"Sorry no, but good guess," he said.

She looked crushed and he wanted to comfort her. As she continued mumbling to herself, she perked up again.

"Alabama," she said.

It was a declaration with a smile that once again he was disappointed he was going to have to shoot down. He didn't know if he could take any more of these highs and lows.

"Sorry," he said, as she looked glum. "How about I just tell you?"

"No, I'm close, I'm sure of it. Although this is a lot harder than I imagined," she said. "I mean, how many more seven letter State names can there be that could also be girls names? I should at least be able to get one right on the next guess, right?"

She looked at him with such hope, he didn't want to crush her enthusiasm and confidence.

"That's right. I bet you'll get it on the next go," he said.

She smiled brightly at him for saying the right words, even if he was lying.

Phoenix was stunned at how Jacqui's face transformed because he said something supportive and encouraging. It made him wonder if she had never been told such words before and the thought made him mad.

He was sitting there trying hard not to chuckle as he watched Jacqui counting and spelling on her fingers and then frown that whatever State she was thinking of definitely didn't have the right amount of letters.

Jacqui was annoyed with herself after thinking she had come up with perfect answer only to find that it was one letter too long.

"Okay, what's got you so annoyed?" he said, curious.

"I thought the answer to one of your sister's names was Virginia, but turns out the stupid State has to be spelt with eight letters and I was wondering if it was possible to lose the R?" she said.

"Somehow I don't think the state of Virginia would be too happy to lose a letter just for my sisters," he chuckled.

"You never know. Maybe they've been spelling it wrong all these years," she laughed.

"Now that would be funny. Unfortunately, unless you're some kind of time traveller that can make the change, it's still eight letters and not seven," he said.

"Fine," she sighed. "Be like that."

He grinned and watched her continue her thinking.

"Okay," she said, hesitant. "I think I might have it, but I seriously don't know if you would name your daughters this.

Montana and Indiana? They're the only ones I can think of which are seven letters."

"You did it," he said. "Yes, those are my older sisters' names."

The full force of Phoenix's smile at her success almost blew Jacqui away. She felt victorious and ecstatic.

"Thank goodness. That's taken me all night. I don't know if I'll even try for the others," she laughed, relieved. "And, I don't want to show my ignorance of just how many places in America I can't name."

"Oh, come on, there's only a few of the tens of thousands of cities in America that they could possibly be named after," he chuckled. "You never know, you might hit it first time."

She liked that Phoenix had a great sense of humour.

"To change the conversation away from my siblings' names, just out of curiosity who set you and Eddie up?" he said, wondering if it was a mutual friend of his and Eddie's. Jacqui was delightful company and this whole dinner had been a very pleasant surprise.

She reddened at having to tell Phoenix the truth.

"Alf, my butcher," she said. "Because of all my terrible man choices."

"Your *butcher* set you up? Wow, you must be very close to have let him do that," he said, astounded and trying to stifle the chuckle wanting to escape.

"Yes," she giggled. "Alf's wonderful. I've known him pretty much my entire life since he's an old friend of my father's. He also has the best fatherly advice and freshest cuts of meat," she said, not mentioning sometimes she wished Alf was her real father.

"A butcher who gives great advice and sets up customers on blind dates. It sounds like a one-stop shop," he grinned. "Tell me, what great advice as he given you?"

"Well, after the drug dealer and before my friend's blind date fiasco he did recommend I stop dating men like I'm buying shoes. I need to be more patient, find someone who fits me perfectly," she said.

Phoenix had to admit it did sound like good advice. Perhaps he could use it on his own younger sisters.

"I have to admit it sounds like a good analogy. Perhaps you can give me his details and I'll stop by whenever I need some sage advice," he grinned.

Jacqui eyed her date closely, looking to see if he was being sarcastic but no, this man actually seemed sincere.

Chapter Five

Tonight hadn't turned out at all like Jacqui expected, but this was just what she needed. Phoenix was a great dinner companion and therefore she didn't miss the loss of Eddie at all. In fact, if Phoenix was the kind of friend Eddie knew, then by her reckoning he must also be a great guy.

"Since my brain is now fried, how about you tell me what you do for a job?" she said.

"I'm a numbers kind of guy," he said.

"An accountant?" she said.

"No, I work in financial investment," he said.

He didn't usually explain in-depth because most women didn't actually care. They just wanted to know his title and then they could assess whether he was rich enough, or making enough money to hopefully be spent on them.

They weren't about to waste their time on a poor, struggling man still trying to climb the corporate ladder.

They wanted the man at the top of the ladder or at least high on it.

After having such a great time and thinking he was such a great guy, now Jacqui was worried about his vague answer. It made her feel like he was into something dodgy and underhanded. Silently she prayed that he wasn't another Allen or some kind of con man.

"So what do you do for a job?" he said.

Fidgeting in her seat she wasn't too sure how honest to be. Normally she'd just say she was an executive assistant.

"I work for the family firm. My father started a company called Aurora Financial Services and now my brother runs it," she said.

Jacqui's answer startled Phoenix so much he couldn't quite hide his surprise, but luckily she didn't notice. How come he had never met or heard of Jacqui before now, if what she said was true? Deciding to ignore the question for now, instead he'd subtly find out the answers he wanted to know.

"So you're an accountant?" he said. It could explain his never having seen her as she was in a different department.

"Yes, I studied and passed the exams, but I'm not practising. At the moment I'm my brother's executive assistant," she said, still annoyed and irritated by Charles wanting to sell Aurora.

Phoenix was thoughtful. He could hear resentment in Jacqui's voice, but didn't know her family so couldn't make a judgement on why she felt the way she did. Unless it was just for the fact she wasn't practising what she studied, which seemed odd. Surely her father or brother would want her to be an accountant in their firm, unless she wasn't a very good one.

"So accountancy's not really your thing? Or are you looking for another job where you can practise?" He knew he was skating on very thin ice and probably came across as nosy.

"Probably a bit of both," she said.

He waited for her to explain in more detail.

"I like accounting, but I don't think I'm passionate about it, and between you and me, my brother wants to sell the business," she said.

The relief she felt now she actually said it aloud, and to someone who looked like they believed her was like a balloon popping and the tension dissipated. She knew she really shouldn't have said anything so confidential, but wasn't it always easier to confide in a stranger?

"Oh?" Now what could he say? If it were true, it could be just the thing his family, including him would be interested in. "You don't think it's a good idea?"

"It's not Charles' thing, I understand that, but to sell something my father worked hard to build up is…" She shook her head in sadness.

"Horrible?" he said, but was really thinking it was only a betrayal unless their father was also in agreement.

She nodded her head.

"Why don't you take over then?" he said.

It was a logical question, he told himself even if he didn't know what kind of person Jacqui was. Would she be a good leader or have the business nous to be able to manage the company?

Once again, she shifted uneasily in her seat and looked at the table refusing to meet Phoenix's eyes as she wished she could disappear. Not knowing whether she should tell him the shameful truth or not, perhaps if she did, then his reaction would show her what his own character was like. Deciding to take a punt on the fact that the man opposite her was nothing like her father, she told him the truth.

"I'm not allowed," she quietly said. "I'm a woman."

Even though Phoenix managed to cover an outraged gasp, he looked angry at her explanation. He had never heard such a ridiculous thing in all his life. He had grown up with four sisters and never once was it mentioned they couldn't do whatever it was they wanted because they were women.

Sure, he and Boston might tease them about certain things, but it was never serious. He supported all his sisters in whatever they did. He wanted to ask Jacqui if she was serious, but could see by the look on her face she was. Was this the real reason she wasn't an accountant in her family's company?

"That is the most ludicrous thing I've ever heard in my life," he said, unable to stop himself raging on her behalf. "Who on earth told you that?"

Exhaling a long breath, she hadn't realised she had been holding while awaiting his answer, she was more than relieved by his reaction. She was also unable to believe someone whom she just met would actually be offended on her behalf and wanted to reach over and kiss him for just saying the words.

"My father is quite… As the head of the family he has very set and old-fashioned ideas. My brother was brought up in the same mould," she said, diplomatic.

"So your own father is the one who said you can't run the business? That if your brother doesn't want it, then to sell?" he said, incredulous. "What about you? Have you told your father?" As soon as the words came out of his mouth, he kicked himself for practically accusing Jacqui of being spineless especially after what she had just revealed. "I'm sorry, I shouldn't have —"

"No, it's okay. Actually I did. I tried. I even…" No, she wasn't going to relive the shameful moment when her father laughed at the thought of her taking over. "Dad said Charles knows what he's doing. However, he did talk to Charles about it because Charles was furious I went behind his back and dad made him agree not to sell for at least a year. I think he's hoping Charles will change his mind. He won't. I don't think he's even going to wait out the year. Knowing Charles, he'd probably slyly get everything arranged so when the year's up it's sold," she said. It was the sort of sneaky and underhanded thing Charles would do.

Phoenix leant back in his chair still trying to comprehend what he just heard, still feeling guilty about his earlier accusatory manner.

"Wow. I can't imagine what it would be like to be my brother's assistant and feel like the family business was being pulled out from under me," he said.

She looked at Phoenix realising he'd just hit the nail on the head. He did seem to understand her predicament.

"Surely your brother needs your father to sign off on the sale of the business, so perhaps that might jolt him into letting you run it," he said.

"He's already signed over everything to Charles a few years ago," she said, shaking her head in dismay.

That would have been around the time Phoenix had joined the company and why he hadn't paid any attention to who was running it because he was too busy trying to get settled and focusing on crushing JJ into oblivion.

"Do you even want to run the company?" he said.

Phoenix's question seemed to come almost like a bolt out of the blue, which seemed silly, but perhaps it was because she had been open about her situation in a way she'd never been before that the question felt like it was taking on a whole new meaning.

Before tonight if anyone had asked the same question she would have automatically answered, "of course".

"I-I don't know," she said. Her answer taking her by surprise and her face must have shown it as her mouth opened and closed before looking a little lost. "I've really never thought about it. I've always been Charles' assistant. I don't want to lose the business, it's very profitable and my family legacy. But…"

"You never thought you would ever have the chance," he said, sympathetic to her plight.

The man sitting across from her was reading her mind so clearly it was a little scary. He was saying the things she had thought deep down or didn't want to acknowledge out loud and bring up to the surface.

"Yes," she said, in all honesty. "I mean I pretty much am now, so even if I did get the title, not a lot would really change."

They continued to make polite conversation over other things like movies and world events, something they both suspected was just to take their minds off Jacqui's confession.

"Oh my God, is that the time? And all I've done is talk your ear off about nothing and solve the names of two siblings," she said, embarrassed, looking at her watch.

"It's fine. I've had a great time and most people would have given up a long time ago or just not really cared that much," he said.

Although she was sceptical about his polite answer, she could feel herself blushing.

"This has been the worst blind date for you, hasn't it? I'm so sorry," she said.

"Why are you sorry? It's been fun, truly," he said.

The sincere smile Phoenix gave her made her stomach flip-flop.

"I'm so jealous you all have such cool names. Well, the three I know, where mine just seems so mundane in comparison," she said.

"Believe me growing up with our names wasn't a walk in the park. We got teased a lot, but now we're adults we like our names a lot more," he smiled.

"So Montana and Indiana are the two eldest, then your brother and you, with two younger sisters bringing up the rear?" she said.

"That's right. Although the two youngest hate the fact they're the youngest and the two oldest like to lord it over all us younger ones because they were named after States unlike the rest of us," he chuckled.

"I wish I had sisters. It must be so great," she said, unable to stop herself from smiling and imagining the arguments.

There was that wistful tone again. It made something deep down in Phoenix's belly tighten in reaction.

"Only if you like constant bickering. Bos and I used to swear mum and dad made sure they had boys in between the girls just to ensure there was a buffer. Girls bicker *a lot* and over every little thing," he said, rolling his eyes at the memories. "And with six children, the variations of fighting can get quite complicated. We have girls versus boys, old versus young, States versus cities, and sometimes it's a complete free-for-all."

"Well, I think it would be fantastic," she smiled.

"Bet you wouldn't think that every time they butt into your life, give you unwanted advice and are generally nosy about every little thing you do, even now," he said.

"Okay, perhaps not that," she said. "But imagine sharing the good times you have together."

"So you're not close to your brother?" he said.

"No. Yes. Sort of. He's my brother and I love him. I even work for him, but he's also quite complex," she said, unable to tell Phoenix just how selfish and chauvinistic Charles could be because that's what he'd learnt from their father. On the other hand, he could also be kind and considerate towards her.

"I know this is going to sound like an odd thing to say, but if you ever need a friendly ear to bash about your family or bad boyfriends, I'm happy to be your sounding board," he said.

The smile which lit up Jacqui's face at his words made tonight's blind date worth it and Phoenix felt like he had somehow won some kind of victory over Eddie. At the thought of his friend, he felt Jacqui was way out of Eddie's league. She was much too classy and dignified for him, or at least that was what he wanted to believe. Then a wave of guilt hit and he decided he should at least try to be a good friend.

"Would you like to give me your phone number so I can pass it on to Eddie? I'm sure he'd be more than happy to arrange another date with you, if that's what you want," he said.

Jacqui felt herself deflate at the polite offer. Something inside her thought Phoenix was lovely even suggesting such a thing, and then something inside her didn't want such a thing at all. She didn't want Eddie, she wanted more of these lovely relaxed dates with Phoenix, only now he brought it up, reminding her he was merely the stand-in. How could she say she didn't give two hoots about Eddie and whether she'd meet him or not.

"Sure, why not? Although I don't want him to feel pressured. Liked I said earlier, I was only doing this for Alf so I don't mind if he's not interested," she said, torn between telling Phoenix she wanted to see him again or just playing it cool. Besides, if she gave him her number then he would also have it and the thought made her happy.

"I'll pass the message on to Eddie and let him decide," he said.

"You're not going to tell him I'm desperate or anything are you?" she said, worried.

"Of course not. But I will mention your buck teeth and hunchback," he chuckled.

"You liar," she gasped, feigning outrage.

"Fine," he sighed. "I'll say nothing except you were delightful company."

"Promise?" she said, still wary.

"Scout's honour," he said, holding up his hand. "However, if he asks me to describe you, I'm telling him about the hunchback."

"Well, that's all right then. Just as long as you don't do it right off the bat. I'd like it to be a surprise if possible," she laughed, rattling off her number and then her phone pinged. It was Phoenix.

"There, now you have my number just in case you need to vent or are so bored that you want to try and solve any more sibling names," he grinned.

Surprisingly, she snapped his photo to go with his number, something she never did. The action took him by surprise, and smiling he did the same.

"So what do you have planned for your weekend?" he said.

"Oh, I'm buying a map," she smiled.

"A map?" he said, perplexed.

"Yes, I need a decent map of America," she said.

Her impish grin made him laugh.

"You do realise there's this thing called the internet and it can easily give you all the information you need?" he said.

"Okay, so I'll print off a map so I can note which places I've suggested, which reminds me, the names of your other siblings aren't in the same States as your two older ones or anyone else's, right?" she said.

"Correct. Would you like to know if they're —"

"No, don't tell me anything," she said, her hands covering her ears. "You said that your brother is a State capital and your two younger sisters were large towns or small cities, right?"

"Right," he nodded.

"Now what did you call him again, I forget," she grinned.

He tapped her nose and smiled.

"Uh-uh, too bad to you. You don't want any help so I'm not going to tell," he said.

She huffed making him laugh.

"It was your rule," he said.

"You didn't have to take it seriously," she said.

"Yes I did, because I bet if I told you, you'd be scolding me for telling you when you wanted to get it all by yourself," he said.

Her scowl told him he was right.

"Don't forget, *four* sisters. I've learnt a lot over the years. You women say one thing, but mean another and either way, I lose. So I'm choosing to stick to *your* rule. Besides, you want another clue, we'll have to have another dinner," he said.

His smile caused her stomach to flutter again. Phoenix looked serious about wanting to catch up with her again and she couldn't help but smile.

"Same time next week?" she said.

He was taken by surprise at the question and then broke into a smile.

"How about we also go somewhere different?" he said.

"Somewhere with a big table to spread out?" she said.

"Huh?" he said, puzzled.

"Well, I will be bringing my map with me," she teased.

"I'm not going through every single city and town," he laughed.

"Oh fine," she huffed, smiling.

"Although, forty-eight states could mean forty-eight dates," he said.

The flickering in his eyes almost made her forget to breathe. She liked the sound of that many dates with Phoenix.

"I think you mean forty-seven," she smiled.

"Huh? There's fifty states, less the two you've already guessed, that leaves forty-eight and you call yourself an accountant," he teased.

"I guess I am the maths whiz between us," she smiled. "You forgot yourself. And since none of you are in the same state that equals forty-seven."

Phoenix laughed at the simple mistake.

"I guess you are the maths whiz. I can't believe I didn't count myself. It's like one of those trick questions they give you," he said.

After making sure Jacqui was safely on her way home, Phoenix went home thoughtful. What started out as an apprehensive blind date turned into a great night, he thought smiling to himself and just thinking about Jacqui made his smile widen.

She was the biggest surprise. Even though she worked in a successful, family-owned company, she was still a down to earth woman, which he liked. Not only that, but he was impressed with her honesty. Then he frowned. What were the odds his blind date would also be with a woman who could possibly technically be his boss. Just remembering her confession made him angry.

Thinking about it, it really wasn't unsurprising that he didn't recognise Jacqui tonight since he was never given her surname and even if he had, it still wouldn't have registered any meaning since he never associated with anyone outside his department except for Tony. While Tony may have referenced Charles Richmond in passing, Phoenix still hadn't realised that there was another sibling working in the company.

There had been many changes in the few short years he had started at Aurora. Tony now was third in charge of the whole of Aurora, with Nelson Fisher taking over as Director of Investments and Phoenix being made the manager of the division. Nelson would have more to do with the Richmond siblings as he attended all the executive meetings.

Now he was wanting to discuss the possibility of Aurora being sold with his family. His phone rang and looking at it, he saw it was his brother. What great timing.

Jacqui went to bed with a big smile on her face thinking of her unexpectedly great time on a blind date with a stand-in blind date or what she could probably call a double-blind blind date or super mystery date. Then she frowned wondering what Phoenix thought about all her terrible confessions. Had she been too honest? Had he been turned off by her family issues and while she hadn't actually openly confessed to enabling her stupid brother for years she still felt guilty about airing the family laundry.

Suddenly panic engulfed her at the thought Phoenix would tell people Charles was thinking of selling? What if clients then began to desert the company in droves? Oh God, she had really messed up and silently prayed Phoenix could be counted on to keep his lips zipped.

If she hid under her covers, was it possible to pretend that part of the night never happened? Then she felt a warm fuzzy feeling inside her, which made her smile as she recalled Phoenix's outrage she wasn't allowed to run the company because she was a woman. Never had Jacqui ever thought someone, a stranger no less, would be so angry on her behalf.

It made her wonder why she had stayed in the job so long? To her shame she knew it wasn't only the extremely exorbitant pay she was getting, it was the fact she secretly told herself she was the brains and without her, the company would be nothing.

If Charles did sell, would the new owners possibly allow her to run it for them, considering she pretty much did now? Then she'd get the accolades and not someone else. Unfortunately she also knew the reality was they'd have their own management team and she'd be out on the street especially since she was a Richmond and they wouldn't want her hanging around any longer than necessary.

If only she could afford to buy the company from Charles, but she didn't have that kind of money or even knew anyone who did, let alone be willing to give her a loan. After all, the company was worth tens of millions of dollars.

Maybe she could gather a group of investors together, and once again she thought of Phoenix and smiled. He said he worked in financial investment so perhaps he could give her some ideas. After all, it wasn't as if she could go to the Aurora investment team and ask them, she giggled to herself.

Her smile widened at managing to find a believable excuse to contact Phoenix even though she hadn't been planning to, or had her subconscious been hoping to?

She went to sleep excited and tomorrow she had a plan to organise.

Monday after work she decided to stop in and see Alf.

"Hi Alf," she smiled.

"What can I do for my favourite customer? How did the blind date go?" Alf said, eager for news.

"He stood me up," she said, trying to look and sound as forlorn and miserable as possible.

The stunned look on Alf's face was priceless.

"What?" he said.

"Supposedly he had a family emergency." She sadly shook her head.

"Oh Jacs, I'm so sorry. Did you at least get dinner?" Guilt

was written all over Alf's face.

"I couldn't sit there all alone looking like a loser. That would have been totally humiliating," she said.

"I'm really sorry it didn't go well. I promise never to set you up again," he said.

"Really?" she said.

"Promise," he said.

"Great," she said, a bright smile coming over her face. "Now, what's good for dinner?"

Alf blinked at Jacqui's instant change in demeanour.

"You played me," he scowled, to her giggle. "Did he really stand you up?"

"Yes. Although in his defence it truly was a family emergency, but he did send a friend to let me know. I ended up eating dinner with them instead and spending your money. So try not to have a heart attack when you see the bill," she said. "*And* now that I have your promise to never set me up ever again, I can keep you on as my butcher."

"So are you going to see Edward?" he said.

"Who knows? His friend did take my number to pass on, but to be honest, I'm not fussed as to whether he calls or not." Saying her thoughts aloud made Jacqui realise she hadn't actually once thought of Edward except for when she initially met Phoenix and received his message and Phoenix kindly offering to pass her number on. Seeing Alf's disappointment, she felt guilty. "Oops, sorry Alf. I didn't mean for it to come out so harsh."

"Want me to set something up again?" Alf winked.

"You just can't help yourself, can you? And after you just promised not to," she laughed. "I think I'll just leave this one to fate. Now, how about some chicken?"

Alf took the hint about the polite change in subject and wrapped up some chicken.

Chapter Six

Phoenix was now in London. After getting Boston's timely call, he explained he had something of the utmost importance he needed to talk to his brother and brothers-in-law about and could they all urgently get together because it was also very confidential.

Yes, it could have been done over the internet, only it wasn't the same as being in the same room as everyone. He also wanted to see his family and get the love and support they all gave each other in person.

Jason lent him the Kwong Lee plane so he could leave first thing in the morning. Fortuitously Lucas and Montana were already in town and brought their kids, so Montana and Indi could catch up and the cousins could see each other. Boston's wife, Alyssa was also going to tag along.

They all agreed to meet at Jason and Indi's house and there was a lot of excited hugging and squealing to see each other again. This was what Phoenix missed being in New York by himself.

"Before we all split up, we have an announcement to make," Boston smiled. "Lys is pregnant."

Everyone in the room beamed as if they already knew before cheers and congratulations along with more hugs and kisses went around.

"This is *so* exciting. We have so much to talk about," Montana said to Alyssa, who looked like she was now caught up in some kind of whirlwind.

"Your timing couldn't have been more perfect, Nix," Boston smiled.

"Do Jack and Frankie know?" Phoenix teased, referring to Alyssa's uncle and father.

"No way. We're not telling them until we have to. They're already constantly on our case and this will just ramp up their meddling even more," Boston said, rolling his eyes.

"I concur. Meddling parents are the worst," Jason said.

"At least with your parents in New Zealand, it's only half as bad," Lucas grinned.

"Once again, I concur," Jason laughed.

Due to the excitement over Boston and Alyssa's news, it took everyone a while to get organised and leave.

The women agreed to stay away for a few hours and then they'd all have quality family bonding time, but should any child be tired and grumpy, they'd be returning earlier so the men better get whatever thing they were doing done or be prepared for a noisy house.

After everyone left and it was just the men, they went into

the lounge and got comfy.

"Okay Nix, you called this urgent meeting so the floor's yours," Jason said.

"You're not in any kind of trouble, are you?" Boston said, concerned.

"No, of course not," he said, but knew from his past behaviour it was a valid question.

"Then what's so urgent?" Boston said.

"You're not getting married, are you?" Jason teased.

"You got someone pregnant?" Lucas said, worried.

"No and definitely no," he laughed, holding up his hands.

The men all looked relieved.

"This stays confidential, right?" he said.

They all nodded and agreed.

"So I met this woman and she tells me Aurora is being put up for sale," he said.

Everyone in the room looked gobsmacked by the news. It was definitely something no one expected Phoenix to say.

"Are you sure?" Jason said.

"Tony hasn't said anything, although I can understand why he hasn't," Boston said.

"Is it legit?" Lucas said. "I'm surprised there hasn't been any whispers."

"I wouldn't have thought Gene would sell. I mean, he started the company. I would have thought that he'd leave it to his children, unless they're not interested?" Jason said.

Surprise coloured Phoenix's face that Jason knew Gene Richmond.

"You know Gene Richmond?" he said.

"Not really, I just know of him. More so because Aurora does the accounts for a few of our little companies over there, and I like to know who I'm doing business with," Jason said, as everyone nodded. "You know, eggs not all in one basket and also, should one of our other accountants not be performing then we've already tested other companies to see what their level of expertise and standard of service is like."

"And here we thought that the KL Corporation always receives the best service," Phoenix chuckled.

"You'd be surprised," Jason grinned. "Some companies get sloppy thinking that they can charge hefty fees and ride the gravy train. We've moved business often because of that."

"I hear you. I'm the same," Lucas said. "Some of the people we've done business with for generations because of their friendships between our grandparents or parents. Then their quality of service slackens off because their children don't care or they just see us as a cash cow who will always be there. It can get quite ugly when you have to move your business and then someone has to explain to the grandparent or parent why our long association with them has been severed."

Phoenix understood that when you're talking the amounts Jason and Lucas were, you needed a lot of trust in the people and company.

"Who's the woman who told you and can she be trusted?" Lucas said, worried someone might be trying to scam Phoenix because they knew he had a wealthy brother and even wealthier brothers-in-law.

“It’s legit,” he said, confident. “It was Gene’s daughter, Jacqueline who told me.”

Once again everyone in the room had the same stunned expressions on their faces.

“You’re sleeping with the boss’ daughter?” Boston said.

“No, dumbo,” he sighed, knowing everyone had the same thought and now he was going to have to tell them the entire story. “If I tell you, do you promise *not* to tell your wives? I don’t need the grief.”

“Aw, come on, Nix. You know the girls will get it out of us and if we don’t tell and then they find out we knew, we’ll *all* be in the doghouse,” Jason moaned, as everyone agreed.

“Well, maybe not Bos,” Lucas chuckled.

“Yes, I won’t be,” Boston grinned.

“Yes, but this is confidential so surely what else I tell you is also confidential,” he said.

“As much as I agree with you, you know the states.” That was the younger siblings nickname for the two eldest Chan sisters. “They’re going to be poking their busybody noses into your *private* life while they have you here and can personally interrogate you,” Boston said.

“They are like bloodhounds. One little whiff of anything romantic and they’ll jump on it,” Lucas laughed.

“Yes, Lucas and I have seen this phenomenon before,” Jason said, shooting a look at Boston.

“Your best shot is to hide behind Bos and Lyssa’s news as long as you can, but even then, you know your sisters won’t leave you alone until they feel you’ve told them *everything* that's happening with you," Lucas said.

"And this is why being part of a big family sucks," Phoenix groaned.

"It's not our fault this family doesn't allow any kind of sibling privacy. You're all up in each other's business," Jason laughed.

"Tell you what, tell us the story and we'll think of a way not to tell the wives. But you know when they return, they'll be not only grilling you, but grilling us about you. And you know the Chan family motto, just be upfront or suffer the wrath of the family on your head," Lucas said, with all the wisdom of years dealing with Montana and her siblings.

"You know he's right, Nix. This family can never keep secrets. They always get out, but we've got your back. The states are going to keep interrogating you until you give it all up. So you might as well front foot it enough to keep them happy, which they will never be," Boston laughed.

"Ain't that the truth," Jason said, raising his glass in salute. "Believe me, we've all been on the end of a Chan family grilling and not even the strongest warriors alive would be able to withstand it. *And* remember you're their *little* brother, so they know all your weaknesses."

"Fine. I can't even believe I'm telling you all this since it's not that big of a deal," he sighed. "I'll just say I came over because of a possible, yet very confidential business opportunity. How's that?"

"Agreed," they all said, knowing it was the truth and their wives wouldn't pry.

"Now back to your *hot* date," Lucas grinned.

"I didn't say it was a date," he scowled.

"So it wasn't?" Jason said.

"Of course it was, *but* it was only one date," he huffed, as everyone laughed.

"That's all you need," Lucas said, as the other's nodded.

Phoenix could see all their wistful faces remembering how they met their wives.

"For goodness sakes, I think you're all getting way too ahead of yourselves." He was trying hard to keep his temper in check, but it was beginning to rapidly rise.

"Fine, tell us all about this *one* date that's not a *big deal* and we'll tell you what an idiot you are and how you're going to end up marrying the boss' daughter," Boston grinned, as once again everyone wore the same look on their faces.

"It was a blind date and not even mine, so there," he snapped. "The only reason I was there was because I was filling in for a friend who couldn't make it because of a family emergency. Jacqui had been set up by her *butcher* of all people."

Three men with silly smiles on their faces just sat there looking at him.

"What?" Phoenix said, bemused.

"If that's not the start to another great Chan love story, I don't know what is," Lucas said, as Boston and Jason nodded their agreement.

"Whatever." Phoenix rolled his eyes.

"Carry on, Nix," Boston said.

As Phoenix explained the date and that he actually hadn't

told Jacqui he also worked at Aurora, he could see everyone's frowns.

"See," he said, finishing his story. "You were all jumping to the wrong conclusion." Now he felt vindicated he was right and everyone else was wrong.

"So let me get this straight, she tells you her idiotic brother wants to sell and you never mentioned you worked for her family?" Jason frowned.

"I know, I should have, but then the rest of the night would have been awkward," he said.

"So you do want to see her again?" Lucas said, as Phoenix shot him a 'well duh' look. "Hey, I'm just asking because you've now come to us straight after a great blind date with news her family's company is for sale. Personally I think it's a great idea we should look into, but it'll all end in tears, especially if you want the girl."

"I didn't say I wanted her," he said, defensive.

"You didn't have to," Jason smiled.

"The fact that you didn't tell her you're in effect her employee because you didn't want to ruin the rest of your *date*, not to mention she was so excited about your siblings and she referred to the next time you meet, just shows how comfortable she must have felt to confide something so confidential," Boston said, trying to hold back his teasing. "I bet you haven't even passed on her number to Eddie."

"Well, I only had dinner with her last night and then I was on a plane here, so I haven't had time to do it," he huffed, but damn his brother for being right. Eddie hadn't even entered his thoughts at all, but that was to be expected, right? After all, he wanted to focus on approaching his family about the sale of Aurora.

"Do you have a photo of her? You do!" Boston laughed, as Phoenix reddened. "I knew it. You've got the hots for her."

"Let's see it," Lucas said.

Sighing and knowing he wasn't going to get any peace until he showed them, he pulled out his phone.

"She's pretty," Jason said.

"Beautiful," Lucas said.

"All right," he scowled, hating the thought they were ogling Jacqui even though they were quite happily married.

"Hm, I remember when I was going through all this with Lys that some smartarse told me this kind of thing would *never* happen to him," Boston teased.

"Looks like the shoe's on the other foot now," Lucas chuckled.

"I remember all of Nix's confident declarations as well," Jason laughed.

"*Nothing* is happening so can we please get back to the problem at hand," Phoenix scowled, to their laughter.

"Which is?" Lucas said.

"I want to buy the company," he said.

Once again everyone's mouths fell open in shock.

"Wow. Didn't see that one coming, did you?" Boston said, looking at his brothers-in-law.

"No," they both said, shaking their heads.

"I just thought he was trying to give us a heads up on a fantastic opportunity before word got out," Lucas said.

"Me too," Jason said.

"Clearly I don't have the money, but I know numbers are my thing and I want my own company someday just like you guys, so what do you think?" he sighed.

The silence was excruciating as he waited for them to respond.

"It's a multi-million dollar company," Lucas said, rubbing his chin.

"And you're young and not experienced enough to know all the ins and outs of running something so large," Jason said.

They were all trying to be tactful and not crush Phoenix's dreams.

"I know," he sighed. "I guess I just saw an opportunity and wanted to jump in feet first like I always do. That's why I wanted to talk to you guys."

"Owning a company like Aurora would be a great addition for the family," Lucas said.

"But how would we do it?" Boston said, wanting to help his brother in any way he could.

"We could look at starting up a family trust or company to buy it," Jason said, rubbing his chin.

Phoenix felt a fluttering of hope, which was then dashed by Lucas' words.

"No offence, Nix, but I'm not sure you're up to the running of such a large and successful company yet. If you had a few more years under your belt or started the company from scratch, it would be different. We'd all be able to see what you can do. If we bought it, I truly can't see putting you in charge straight off the bat. It would be too risky," he said.

Phoenix deflated knowing Lucas was right. These men were all being nothing but honest, and the weight of knowing they invested a lot of money would be a very heavy burden on his shoulders. Therefore he wouldn't want to screw it up in any way.

"What about if we install someone as a caretaker CEO who can teach Nix as well. Then when he's ready to assume the helm, he can take over?" Jason said.

"It's doable. What do you think, Nix? Are you willing to put in the hard yards and wait?" Boston said, knowing that although his brother had mellowed over the years and wasn't as quick to rush in, he could still be impatient.

"It could take years," Lucas said, not wanting to raise Phoenix's expectations that he'd be running it within a year. With a company like Aurora, it would bring complexities Phoenix had no experience at all in dealing with as an overall CEO.

Knowing his family were trying to find a happy compromise for him made Phoenix's heart swell. He truly was lucky to have such a wonderful family and as much as Lucas' comment chafed because he wanted to be running the company as soon as possible, he also knew Lucas spoke the truth.

"You know I'll work every spare minute of the day to repay your faith and to keep making this company a success," he said, feeling buoyed with hope once more.

"That's the thing, Nix. We actually don't want you to do that," Lucas said.

"What?" There seemed to be a shocked echo around the room in reaction.

"Calm down, everyone. All I meant is we also want you to ensure that you also have a personal life, Nix. We don't want you burying yourself in work just to try and prove yourself. You deserve a personal life as well. I think we're all in agreement when I say," Lucas eyeballed his brothers-in-law. "That we'd rather you go slow and have a well-balanced life than just concentrating on work."

Everyone seemed to exhale a sigh of relief at Lucas' wisdom.

"That's true, Nix. We don't want you burning out or having no life. You're young and deserve to have time out and fun. The company will always be there," Jason said. "And a company can't keep you warm at night."

"Besides if you play this right, then perhaps you and Jacqui will be having office shenanigans every now and then," Boston teased, making kissing noises as everyone laughed and Phoenix could only smile.

"I don't know what to say. I mean, I know how you supported Bos, but to have you guys try and do the same for me is actually quite overwhelming," he said, emotional.

They stood and hugged.

"Nix, you're our brother. Of course we'd support you," Boston said.

"Besides, having a company like Aurora in the family makes great business sense, personally and professionally. We also expect you to make us even richer, like you're already doing with your investment tips," Jason laughed.

"It's what family does," Lucas said. "Look at how all of our families have helped various extended family members out at different times when they needed help."

It was true. Although they were connected because of the Chan siblings, it wasn't unheard of to get extended family to assist if they could, like Kai helping Alyssa's father.

"You guys are the best," Phoenix said, wiping his eyes.

"Yes, we are," Lucas grinned.

"So what do we do now?" he said.

"Well, I'm thinking if this is still all very hush-hush, that makes us probably one of the first to know. We have two choices: try and tie this all up before anyone else gets wind of it and a bidding war happens, or we just wait and hope for the best," Jason said. "Personally I vote for option one."

"Me too. We don't really want to be in a bidding war," Lucas said.

"But what if Jacqui finds out I'm the one who spilled the beans?" Phoenix said, worried.

That's when Boston knew his little brother truly liked this woman, even if he was in denial about it. Normally Phoenix would have been full steam ahead and worried about Jacqui's reaction later. After it was too late and everything was done and dusted.

"Why don't we subtly sound Charles out?" Boston said. "I've got some work to do over in New York, perhaps I can visit Tony to catch up and hopefully happen to run into Charles."

"But won't people be suspicious since you're my brother?" he said.

"Okay, how about this, let's work on how to structure the company and the finance. When that's sorted we can sound out Charles and have a viable offer as well. That way, if he wants to take it, it's ready to go. If news gets out first, then we'll have to rethink it all," Lucas said.

"We'll all keep in touch. But Nix, for now, I think you're better staying out of it. The less you know, the better," Jason said.

Although Phoenix was hurt by the suggestion, after a moment's thought he realised Jason was right. He didn't want to have to lie if he saw Jacqui again and the knot in his stomach he hadn't realised was there was now getting bigger. He only hoped she wouldn't see that his family buying her family's company as a betrayal, yet highly doubted it.

"The girls will be back shortly, so I suggest we just chill and watch some sport before their return and the noise level not only goes up, but the grilling starts," Boston said, looking at his watch.

"I hope you brought your fire retardant suit, Nix," Jason chuckled.

"Yes, it's about to get hot and not for us," Lucas teased.

Phoenix flipped them the bird as they all laughed.

As predicted, no sooner had the wives and children returned and told everyone how their outing went and kids who needed naps were put down and others were given snacks, the grilling started.

Phoenix felt like he was some sort of rotisserie over a fire pit being agonisingly slowly spun around and around from all the seemingly never-ending questions. None of his answers seemed to satisfy his sisters and as he looked to Boston and their brothers-in-law for help, they all not only grinned, but pretended not to notice.

"I still can't believe you made a surprise visit," Indi said, sensing there was more to his visit.

"Yes, and then spent time alone with the boys," Mon said.

"I just missed you guys and I needed a little man time with my family. There's nothing wrong with that, is there?" he said.

"Well, that settles it. There's only one reason for all this," Indi grinned.

"There is?" Alyssa said, confused.

"Of course. It's girl trouble otherwise why else would we be sent away?" Indi said, happy at solving the mystery.

"Like I said, I missed my family," he said, hating how accurate Indi was.

"Liar. Indi's right. If it was missing us, and I believe part of you does, you wouldn't have us sent away. We *all* would have spent the day together," Montana said. "So spill, who is she and how did you meet?"

"I also had confidential business opportunity to discuss with the boys," he said.

The women all looked to their husbands who nodded, yet remained silent.

"I don't know…" Montana frowned. "It seems legit but still…"

"Was it a cute-meet as they say these days?" Indi smiled.

"I hope it's a good story," Alyssa said. "Everyone in this

family seems to have a good story."

"It was *one date*," he scowled, before silently kicking himself really hard after realising he accidentally let the cat out of the bag himself.

"Oh my gosh, we're getting a new sister-in-law," Indi and Montana squealed, as they jumped around hugging each other and then Phoenix, to his disgust, at their overreaction.

All the men just laughed at the sisters' reactions.

"Boys, has Nix told you we're getting a new sister-in-law," Indi crowed.

"This is so exciting," Montana gushed. "Tell us all about her."

"Oh my God, talk about an overreaction," he scowled.

It didn't matter what he did or said, as he had been previously warned, his sisters and Alyssa ganged up on him squeezing every little detail out of him.

"What's her name?"

"How'd you meet?"

"What does she look like?"

By the end of his story there were three sets of sighs.

"Now I wish I had been on more blind dates. It's so romantic," Montana sighed.

"Hey, our first date was kind of a blind date," Lucas said.

"Not really, but okay," she said, kissing him.

"Would you call our first meeting a blind date, Jase?" Indi said.

The heat from his eyes in remembrance made her shiver.

"I guess so, since we didn't even know each other's names before we —"

She quickly covered his mouth as her cheeks reddened in mortification, and even though everyone knew the story, Indi still got embarrassed by it.

"Ours wasn't a blind date," Boston smiled.

"It could be since we didn't know each other." Alyssa smiled lovingly at her husband.

"It was love at first sight," he said, kissing her as everyone nodded their agreement, as it also applied to them and their spouses, making Phoenix envious.

"Although I do have to admit I still don't quite get how Nix's *one* date equals future wife," Alyssa said, confused.

"Have we taught you nothing?" Montana teased.

"Yes, Lys. All of our *first* meetings have been more than memorable for various reasons," Indi said. "In which they all end in happily ever after."

Alyssa still didn't quite seem to understand.

"Of course, we'll know for sure when we find out just what mess he's got himself tangled up in. That's the real clincher," Montana said.

"Hey, I'm right here, you know," Phoenix huffed.

"So what have you got yourself tangled up in with *Jacqui*?" Indi said, eyeballing him.

Suddenly he wished he never opened his mouth and brought their attention back to him.

"There is *no* mess," he said, defensive.

"Sure there's not," Montana grinned. "You rush over here for 'family' time and a confidential business opportunity just after meeting Jacqui and there's no mess? Have you not heard our stories? We make nothing but messes, which then have to be sorted before true love prevails."

Again, he just huffed his response.

"Don't worry, Lucas will tell me," Montana winked.

"And Jase will tell me," Indi grinned.

Both women looked at Alyssa.

"What? I thought it was a given Boston would tell me," she said.

"Being a part of this family is all about being nosy, giving your unwanted two cents and loads of teasing," Indi laughed.

"Oh, in that case, you know Boston will tell me," Alyssa giggled.

"Atta girl. You're becoming more of a Chan every day," Indi smiled.

"By the time we've managed to sort out Nix's love life and gotten him married, you'll be a dab hand when it comes to Vanna and Lexi," Montana said.

"Won't they be annoyed their sister-in-law is giving them stick and putting her nose in their business?" Alyssa said, worried. Although she loved having sisters since she was an only child, nevertheless she also didn't want to make any of them angry at her.

"No, we all do it. Besides, Nix and Bos will probably end up doing it for you so you can play good cop when they moan about the boys being overbearing and overprotective," Montana said.

"We are not," Phoenix huffed, to Boston's agreement.

"Sure, you're not,' Indi smiled.

Chapter Seven

On Monday, Phoenix received a text from Jacqui seeing if he was free to meet up. Admittedly, he was surprised to hear from her so soon and was unable to hide his smile seeing her photo pop up on his phone. Nonetheless he was glad she had gotten in touch with him as he had been trying to think of an excuse to see her again.

Remembering what she said on their date and not wanting to make her uncomfortable, he decided to not only meet her at a restaurant, but also asked for a table of four. This way, should she have brought a map of America with her, it could be spread out.

Jacqui was on tenterhooks ever since Phoenix texted back agreeing to dinner and naming the place. It wasn't what she'd expected and yet, it felt special. She didn't know why she felt like that, but she did.

She also made sure to dress to impress knowing she was

meeting him after work and wore her favourite faux-suede chocolate brown skirt with a blouse. Classy, but not too dressy. All day she dithered over whether Phoenix would like what she was wearing and then she'd get mad at herself for even caring what he thought. She liked her clothes and wasn't trying to impress him, she'd firmly tell herself, even though she really was.

She printed out a list of all the State capital names so she could grill him about his siblings, and a couple of maps of the country. She also brought along a pad and pen to make any notes and then realised it might be a little over the top and yet, she couldn't quite make herself leave them behind. If worse came to worse, she'd lie and say that she always carried a notepad and pen in her handbag. In a last minute attack of anxiety, she also threw a highlighter into her bag, pretty sure she wouldn't need it, but it never hurt to be prepared, just in case.

Seeing Phoenix in a suit made her stomach flutter and she silently hoped that he also liked what he saw.

"You look lovely," he smiled.

Cue more fluttering and heartbeat acceleration at his compliment.

"Thank you. How was your day?" she said.

He wondered if now was the time to own up to the fact she was technically his boss, but he didn't want to ruin dinner and at the same time, he didn't want to lie.

"Not bad, busy as always. How was yours?" Chicken, he scolded himself.

"Busy too. I'm surprised they seated us at a table for four

since there's only two of us and they seem to be quite busy." she said, as they sat and waited for their food,

"Actually I asked for this just in case," he said, pink stealing up his neck to his cheeks.

"You did? Why?" she said.

The surprise in her voice now made him feel stupid for even thinking that she'd bring a map. Clearly she had only been teasing and making polite banter.

"I, er, thought you might have brought a map and a table for two wouldn't have really let you spread out," he said, embarrassed.

"Oh, thank God you brought it up," she said, relieved. "I didn't want to seem like a right weirdo if you know, that joke was just for one night."

She pulled out all her stuff out of her bag and he chuckled.

"Wow, you've really come prepared and put a lot of thought into this," he said.

Secretly he was pleased she remembered and this was just the thing to put them both at ease. A distraction from the fact that they were on their second date.

"Now I'm thinking I go through all the State capitals first, it'll be quicker and then I'll have narrowed it down to four names," she said.

"Sounds like a plan," he said.

She began rattling off names in State alphabetical order and as he said, "no," she crossed it off her list.

"Boston?" she said, now almost half way through the list and feeling like the whole idea was a failure.

"Bingo," he smiled.

"Boston? Truly? Your brother's name is Boston?" she said, torn between being sceptical as Phoenix might be lying and excited she had finally guessed another name.

"Yes," he laughed. "I can't see why you'd think I'd be lying about it."

"Well, I don't know," she huffed. "You might be thinking this is just dragging on and so you said yes, when really his name is Tallahassee or Topeka."

"Again, why would I lie about his name? If it was Tallahassee or Topeka I'd definitely wait until you said those before confirming it. The look on your face would have been priceless. Can you imagine? Yes, my brother's name is Tallahassee Chan. You'd be right to be sceptical on that one," he said, unable to stop laughing at the thought of Boston being called Topeka Chan or even Tally Chan for short. He'd probably change his name to John if that was the case.

"Since you put it like that, I'm sorry for insinuating you were lying," she said.

"Don't worry about it. I got a good laugh out of it," he said.

Jacqui was pleased Phoenix wasn't mad at her and had a great sense of humour. Even she couldn't understand why she would have even thought he was lying about his brother's name since there was really no need to.

"So now I've got Montana, Indiana, Boston and Phoenix," she said, pulling out her maps to show him. "Here's a couple of maps I printed off. Can you look at them and tell me if you at least see your younger sisters' names on them? That will at least narrow it down a little, otherwise I'm going to have to print off each state and we'll be going on forty-six dates so on each one I can run through all the names of that State, unless of course, I happen to strike it lucky and get it in two, which would be a minor miracle I'd say," she said.

Phoenix wondered if he should lie just to be able to keep seeing Jacqui.

While he was reading, Jacqui wondered if she hoped the names were on there or not. Her idea of forty-six dates with Phoenix wasn't a bad one. It was also a great excuse to continually meet up with him.

Now that she got the chance to look at him properly, once again she felt her stomach flutter. He was clearly Asian with the most dreamy accent, his jet black hair was cut stylishly short and suited his face. She thought he was not only very handsome, but very photogenic. He was taller than her, but not by much and in heels they were pretty much the same height, which she liked because then she could see into his beautiful caramel eyes. His eyelashes were long and she envied him for those.

In a suit, he looked svelte and when he had taken off his jacket, she noted his shirt showed hints of a well-toned torso underneath, something she hadn't noticed last time, but that would have been because she had been too busy being nervous about having a date with a random stranger.

At the beginning of dinner tonight she was wound so tight with nerves thinking about how she was going to broach her idea of getting a group of investors to buy Aurora and couldn't help but be relieved he brought up her bringing a map. It was a great distraction and gave her some breathing space and a chance to relax, but now her nerves had returned in full-flight.

Would he laugh her out of the restaurant at her idea or would he think it was a good one? What if he took her idea and then cut her out of it? What did she really know about Phoenix Chan except he was from New Zealand, had five siblings, was handsome and made her stomach flutter? Nothing. A big, fat nothing.

Perhaps she should just use this date to gather more information about him first before she floated her idea. Yes, that was a better idea. She ignored her brain telling her she was only using this as an excuse so she would have yet another reason to see him again.

He looked up from his reading and smiled and Jacqui felt her heartbeat quicken and there was that fluttering sensation again.

"You're in luck, their names are on both sheets," he said.

She blinked and had to quickly cover over the fact that she hadn't quite been listening.

"I'll compare both sheets and then I can narrow it down," she said.

She grabbed her pen and he stopped her as she stared at his hand on top of hers.

"How about we celebrate the victory of getting one more name for tonight. If I let you carry on, I might as well be sitting here by myself and that's not as pleasant as having you to talk to," he said.

She melted at his smooth talking, but wasn't that what she wanted, to get to know him better?

"Okay, so what do your brother and sisters do for a living?" she said.

Silently he groaned. Him and his big mouth had now opened a can of worms. He'd learnt over the years not to mention just who his siblings were married to, as some women seemed to think he too was wealthy like his brothers-in-law, when nothing could be further from the truth.

Clearly he couldn't really hide being Boston's brother, but even that wasn't so bad until Boston's company became so successful there were numerous articles written about him.

"The two younger ones are looking to spread their wings very shortly. Lexi is about to do her OE in England," he said.

"OE?" she said, puzzled.

"It stands for overseas experience. That's what we Kiwis call going off to see the world, usually to England," he said.

"Oh, okay. So what about your two eldest sisters then?" she said.

"My two older sisters are both married with children and are happy housewives. My brother owns his own company," he said.

"Wow. So would your brother expect his wife to stop work when they have children?" She hoped and prayed Phoenix and his brother weren't like that. There was no way she was going to be a stay-at-home mother, subject to the whims of her husband. She saw what that kind of life did to her own mother.

"I don't know," he frowned. "I guess that's up to Lyssa. What about you? Would you want to be a stay-at-home mother if you could?"

"Hell no," she said, vehement.

The strength of her answer took him aback until he remembered Jacqui had said her father was chauvinistic, and didn't think women were capable of running a business. Therefore, her answer made a lot of sense.

"And if my husband expects me too, then he's got another thing coming. If he wants someone to stay at home and take care of the kids, he can," she said.

"Fair enough," he said, to her surprise.

"You wouldn't mind?" she said.

"I'm all for my wife to keep working as long as one of us can also be around for our children, so why not? We can also have a nanny," he said.

"Wow, I think you may be the first man I've ever met that's ever thought like that," she said.

"Ah, but don't forget, you've been a bad judge of men," he teased.

"Doesn't that include you?" she said.

"No, because not only was our meeting a set-up by your own *butcher*, but I was the last minute stand-in. So unless Eddie was also one of those kinds of men, which I'm pretty sure he isn't, then I may possibly have been too," he said.

A tug of guilt ate away at him that he still hadn't passed Jacqui's number onto Eddie.

"You make a good point. Maybe everyone who is unlucky in love should be set-up by their butcher. It would make the world a better, more loving place," she grinned.

"Maybe it'll be a new reality TV show, *Blind Date Butchery*," he chuckled.

"That's a terrible name. It sounds like something out of a horror movie," she said, screwing up her face.

"Which is why I'm not in television, which reminds me, what did you need to talk to me about?" he said.

"Oh, I forgot," she lied.

Phoenix didn't know why Jacqui just lied, but since he wasn't exactly being truthful either, he decided to let it slide. After all, perhaps it was better just not to know.

Chapter Eight

Nonsensical jibberish. These were the only words Phoenix could think as incessant chatter washed over him. It wasn't Stan's fault, as he was only a baby, who was happily smiling and chatting to his favourite uncle, and Phoenix couldn't help but smile back.

"Hi buddy," he crooned, scooping up the little boy to give him a big cuddle and blow raspberries on his skin thus making Stan giggle and wriggle with glee.

His best friend in this metropolis of a city, Cameron walked into the room and enjoyed the sight of seeing his friend and son smiling.

It was Boston who got Phoenix in touch with a friend, who then put him in touch with his younger cousin, Cameron, who was also living the bachelor lifestyle in New York. This was to give Phoenix someone to show him the ropes until he got settled.

The two young men out on the town had some great times together becoming so close, Phoenix was even Cameron's best man at his wedding to Jennifer and godfather to his son, Stan.

"Hey Nix, glad you could make it. Where's Jen?" he said, looking around for his wife.

"Done a runner. Said you'd be fine since I'm here to help out." Phoenix smirked, putting Stan back down on the floor so he could crawl around.

"More like she didn't want to spend any more time looking at your ugly face," Cameron said, with an easy banter. "Actually, she knew I wanted to talk to you alone."

The serious look on Cameron's face put Phoenix instantly on his guard, not knowing if it was good or bad.

"What's up?" he said, as Cameron passed him an ice-cold beer.

"You remember Jen's Aunt Mabel? In her sixties, plump, married to Randy and quite a personality. Said to you at our wedding that you should get rid of the 'skinny, bony redhead because even her big boobs couldn't help make her any smarter'?" Cameron chuckled, jogging his friend's memory.

Phoenix not only liked Mabel's blunt in your face honesty, but the older lady had been right about Shari. However, Phoenix hadn't been dating her for her intelligence.

"What about her?" he said, merely out of curiosity.

"Well, Mabel's got a friend whose daughter needs a better love life," Cameron said, as a loud groan reverberated around the room.

"Why me?" he said, ambushed. "What have I done to deserve this? Have I not been a good enough friend to you? Do I not see my godson enough? Should I have made some sort of pass at Jen back in the early days so she'd think I'm some sort of sleaze. Is that why she's punishing me now?"

Seeing Phoenix being melodramatic, Cameron couldn't help but grin over his beer.

Cameron remembered the day his cousin, Sam told him he had given Cameron's number to his friend Boston's brother who had transferred to New York. Cameron hadn't been keen to be saddled with some random stranger and moaned to Sam about it.

When his phone rang, his first thought was the man on the other end of the line wasn't English like he expected and the second thought was the man was just as hesitant about being given Cameron's number.

Deciding to do the right thing, he agreed to meet up with Phoenix if only to give him some advice on where things were et cetera. But when they met at a sports bar, he was surprised to find Phoenix was nowhere near English. He was Chinese and from New Zealand of all places.

Over some beers, Cameron ended up taking Phoenix under his wing as they enjoyed each other's company bantering about sports teams and other things so much so, Cameron decided maybe this stranger wasn't such a bad person after all.

Now here they were, best friends and Cameron knew Phoenix wasn't the kind of guy to boast about being related to two of the world's richest families even if it was through his sisters' marriages. He also knew how hard it must have been for Phoenix to even broach the subject of money to his own family because he wasn't the flashy arrogant kind of guy with confidence up the wazoo like some people they knew, who would've had no shame in doing just that.

Phoenix was also the epitome of a best friend that anyone could ever possibly want. He was honest and loyal and Cameron had lost count at how many times Phoenix had dropped his plans to help him and Jen out when they were in a bind. Phoenix didn't have to do it, yet he did, and so Cameron thought of his friend more like a brother and hoped this whole thing with Jacqui and Aurora ended well.

He had only agreed to persuade Phoenix to go on the blind date because of who the woman involved was and knew Phoenix would be delighted. Not that he was going to tell his friend that.

"Would you believe it's because Jen thinks, and I totally disagree by the way, that you're great dating slash boyfriend material?" Cameron chuckled.

"Well, you tell Jen that she's wrong," he smiled, holding up his beer in salute to the absent woman.

Phoenix liked Jen a lot and was happy she and Cameron got married, but to hang him out to dry like this? He was going to have to rethink his opinion of her.

"So what does this have to do with Mabel pimping me, someone she's only met once, out to be someone's blind date?" he said.

"Since our wedding, it seems Mabel's taken a real shine to you. You made a real impression on her and she always asks after you," Cameron grinned. "First it was to know if you had got rid of the bony redhead and from then on, every time we see her she always asks what you've been up to. She likes to hear about your parade of women. It gives her a good laugh."

"Really?" He wasn't sure if he should be flattered he was memorable to the woman or not. "Well, I hope you make up some good stories for her," he grinned.

"Of course," Cameron chuckled. "Not only is she a favourite aunt, it also puts me even more into her good books."

"Wow, my best friend's just using my life to win brownie points with Jen's aunt. That's friendship for you," he said, then shook his head. "I still can't believe you'd let Jen do this to me."

"I tried to tell her, but it seems she's got a bee in her bonnet about you being the right man for the job. So, man enough?" Cameron's eyes were not only mischievous, but held a silent dare.

Silently Phoenix was cursing his best friend to hell and Cameron knew it.

"Fine. *One date*. That's it. And you tell your sneaky wife next time to do her own dirty work," he scowled, tossing back the remainder of his beer.

With that settled, the two men chatted and watched sports on TV.

Later, Jen hesitantly entered the room unsure whether Phoenix would agree to go on a blind date with her Aunt Mabel's friend's daughter, Jacqui.

"Is it safe to come in?" she said, looking warily at Phoenix for an answer.

"Yeah, chicken, it is," he scowled.

"Oh good, so you got him to agree?" she said, to her husband.

"All it took was a dare," Cameron grinned.

"So you don't want the gold seats to the Rangers on Thursday?" she said, sitting on her husband's lap.

Cameron groaned and Phoenix stared at his friend.

"What gold seats?" he said.

"Great one, hon. I was using that as a bribe for the next thing I needed him to do for me," Cameron said.

"Sorry," she said, contrite and kissing his cheek.

"What tickets?" Phoenix said, knowing Jen had connections for all sporting events in New York and couldn't believe his best friend was holding out on him.

"Jen got two gold seating tickets to Thursday's game and I need a *teeny* little favour from you."

Phoenix wasn't impressed at all with his friend.

"*What?*" he scowled.

"We need you to babysit so we can have a romantic night out," Cameron said, to Jen's adoring look at her husband.

Phoenix tried not to be envious of his friend's icky lovey-dovey display of affection.

"God, if it'll get you to stop that, *fine*," he sighed, yet they both knew he would always have done it.

The game had come back on and soon all thoughts of blind dates and babysitting were forgotten.

Jacqui didn't know how she managed to let her mother talk her into a blind date with her good friend, Mabel's niece Jen's friend. It was a mouthful just trying to say the connection between them. All she knew was his name was Nick and he was going to be holding a rose. Silently praying there weren't going to be too many men entering the restaurant holding a rose, otherwise she could end up making quite an idiot of herself.

It had been a surprise when she went to visit Fleur Richmond, more to moan about her father and brother, that her mother brought up Jacqui's love life.

"Jacqui, Mabel swears she's found you the perfect man," Fleur said, with a big smile on her face.

"Oh mum," she sighed. "I'm fine."

"No, you're not. And don't think I don't know you've been in and out of relationships like a revolving door," Fleur said.

Alarm bells started ringing that Fleur seemed so certain she knew about her daughter's disastrous love life.

"Who have you been talking to?" Jacqui said, her eyes narrowing with suspicion.

"No one," Fleur said, looking guilty.

"*Mum*," she said.

"Oh fine," Fleur sighed. "I ran into Alf, okay? And I have to say that it hurts he seems to know more about your love life than I do."

"It's not like that, mum," she said, trying to placate her and shoo away the feelings of guilt that it was true. "It's just I see him more often and we chit-chat, that's all."

"And yet, you let *him* set you up on a blind date?" Fleur said.

The accusation stung and Jacqui silently cursed Alf and his blabbermouth. Wait until she saw him again, she'd be giving him a piece of her mind.

"That doesn't mean you and Mabel get to try and do the same thing," she said.

"Well, we wouldn't if you not only kept me in the loop, but actually managed to find a great boyfriend. One that isn't into drugs," Fleur chided.

Once again Jacqui cursed Alf's big mouth. Yes, she was definitely having words with her butcher on her next visit or just to fix him, she wouldn't even patron his shop any more. No, she couldn't do that because she like him too much.

"It wasn't like that. That all happened after we split up," she said, to no avail.

"It's already set and you will meet Nick at Mateo's at seven. He'll be holding a rose for you to recognise him," Fleur said.

"But mum, what's wrong with this man he can't find his own date, let alone the fact he's a friend of Mabel's niece's. It's just creepy. What if he's some kind of serial killer? Wouldn't you feel really guilty if I disappeared? My body was found dumped in the river?" she said, melodramatic, but she didn't need her mother or Mabel's help. Especially not now when she might have a chance with Phoenix.

"Please Jacs, just this once. I feel like I've let you down," Fleur said.

Seeing the sadness on her mother's face, Jacqui knew this

wasn't just a ruse to guilt her into the date. Her mother truly felt guilty.

"Oh mum, you've never let me down," she said.

"If only I had stood up to your father more about the way he treated you." Now Fleur was in tears and so was Jacqui. "I feel like it's my fault you can't find the right boyfriend, because of your father," she said.

"No mum, it's not that. Believe me, I just haven't found him yet, that's all. Promise," Jacqui said.

That seemed to cheer her mother up a little as they both wiped their eyes.

"I do only want what's best for you, you know," Fleur said.

"I know," she said. "Mum, you know Charles is planning on selling the company, don't you?"

She decided to tell her mother the truth, not that Fleur had any say in the matter but still, she was their mother and deserved to be kept up with the news, as she tried to ignore the guilt she felt over how her mother found out about her love-life.

"Charles has never liked working there, not even when he was younger, so I'm not surprised. I'm just surprised Gene hasn't gone ballistic over it," Fleur said.

"He sort of did when I told him, but then he reverted back to the fact Charles knew best," she said.

Fleur sighed. It was one of the reasons she finally decided to divorce him after decades of marriage, her ex-husband just couldn't see their son's flaws in anything. He was too set in his ways to ever change.

"You know, it took me years to realise you did your brother's homework," Fleur said.

"You knew?" she said, surprised by the revelation.

"No." Fleur shook her head. "Not until you became his executive assistant and never went and became an accountant in your own right, did I realise. I'm so sorry, honey."

Somehow her mother's confession made her release the tension she'd been holding in all these years.

"Did you know I confessed to dad I've been doing all Charles' work and running the company for years, and even told him I would run the company if Charles doesn't want it," she said.

"Let me guess, he didn't believe you or made Charles out to be a genius in hiding the truth," Fleur sighed, knowing her husband hadn't changed one little bit.

"That's exactly right," she said.

"Sometimes I wish you would just resign from the company and let Charles flounder and then your father would finally see the truth," Fleur said, surprising Jacqui. "Then I realised Gene would just rationalise it away because if he had to acknowledge Charles wasn't as smart as he wanted him to be, then he'd also have to admit to what a failure his son is to himself. And I think that's the one thing your father would never be able to accept."

Jacqui nodded, realising her mother was right. Her father would never be able to accept Charles was a failure or less than what he wanted him to bc.

"I'm so glad we had this talk, mum," she said.

Mother and daughter hugged and for Jacqui it seemed like a weight had been finally lifted off her shoulders. At least one of her parents could see her as her own person and that she was smart and capable.

"Me too, honey, me too. And, I think we should have a mother daughter day. Let's go shopping," Fleur laughed.

"Why not? Let's go," she said, happy.

It turned into a great day with Fleur picking Jacqui out a dress for her blind date, not that Jacqui wanted anything new. She had plenty of clothes in her closet, but sensing it would make her mother happy, she agreed which was why she was now wearing a lovely emerald green wraparound dress in Mateo's.

To try and distract herself from the nerves and torture of waiting she pulled out a map of America to study.

She also tried hard to dismiss any guilt she felt about being on a blind date tonight. She wasn't cheating on Phoenix because they weren't in a relationship or even dating and yet, it still felt like she was.

Chapter Nine

Phoenix honestly didn't know how he got himself into these ridiculous situations, he thought as he entered the restaurant of his latest blind date. Never in his life had he ever been on so many blind dates. To be honest, he had never been on a blind date in his life until now. Although he couldn't exactly quite count the one for Eddie as him going on it since it was meant for his friend.

It was his nervousness, which made him take a deep breath before entering the restaurant and going straight up to the maître d', not even looking around to see if he could see anyone who looked like they might be waiting for him.

Before he could even ask about a reservation, the hairs on the back of his neck prickled as a voice he recognised spoke.

"Phoenix? Is that you? What are you doing here?" Jacqui said, surprised to see him.

Stifling a groan as pink crept up his neck at being caught

out on another blind date by Jacqui of all people, he turned and saw himself staring at the most beautiful woman in the world.

It wasn't as if she had given herself a makeover or anything, nevertheless this time something just seemed to hit him harder.

"Jacqui, you look gorgeous. I'm here on a date, what about you?" he said, trying hard not to sound or look guilty, or wanting to say it was a blind date. That made him feel even more like he was cheating on her, because that was their 'thing', he thought to himself.

"Oh, I'm here on a date also," she said, wanting the ground to swallow her whole, noting Phoenix was not only also here on a date, but didn't seem too upset to see her at the same restaurant as well. Clearly she made the previous two times she dined with him out to be a lot more in her head than in his. He had just been friendly and she was the one who had stupidly begun to weave fantasies about him.

He looked around relieved he didn't see another man with her because he would have been very tempted to punch them before ordering them to leave Jacqui alone. She was his. But then how would he explain his own hypocrisy?

"Is your date just parking the car?" he said, hoping her date might have fallen down an imaginary well.

"Actually, I'm on a blind date," she blushed.

Her cheeks were rosy pink as he looked gobsmacked by her confession. Was that good or bad?

"So am I," he said.

"Really?" she said.

The surprise on her face, made him want to laugh and scowl at the same time. Jacqui was blind date cheating on him, yet wasn't he doing the exact same thing?

"Yes, really. Who's your date with?" he said. Was it too much to dare to hope it was him?

"His name is Nick and he was supposed to be coming with a rose," she said.

He looked down at his hands as if seeing them for the first time.

"Oh my God, I forgot the rose in the taxi," he said.

"It's a shame your name isn't Nick," she said, regretful. "What's the name of your date?" She was only asking to be polite, since she didn't really want to know.

"Actually I don't know. I was never given a name. I was just told my friend Jen's, Aunt Mabel decided to set me up with her good friend's daughter," he said, slightly distracted, wondering if he could find a florist open at this time of night.

"Did you say Mabel set you up?" she said, stunned.

"Yes. Why?" he said, confused.

She burst into laughter, puzzling him by her reaction.

"I'm your date. How do you even know Mabel?" she said.

"I don't really, and considering I only met her once years ago, I have no idea why she thought of me," he said, although suspected it was because of Cam's stories about him. He also didn't know if his friend knew Jacqui would be his date tonight or not, if he did, there'd be payback. "I was just told I was going on a blind date. So you're truly my blind date?"

"Yes, and you're *Nick*," she smiled.

"I am?" he said, confused.

"I have a funny feeling *Nix*, got a little lost in translation," she giggled.

"I still don't understand how I'm Nick or your blind date, not that I'm unhappy about it," he smiled.

"My mother and Mabel are good friends," she said.

The look of understanding on Phoenix's face made her laugh even more.

"Well, it looks like I'm actually going to owe Mabel for this," he said. "Sorry, but I forgot the rose in the taxi."

"Don't worry about it. It looks like I owe my mother one, too. I tried to get out of tonight, you know, but she managed to manipulate me into coming," she said.

"Well, I for one am ecstatic she did, otherwise I'd be the one sitting here tonight looking like an idiot," he chuckled.

"I would have sent a stand-in," she giggled.

"I'd rather have the real thing," he said.

The heat from his eyes made her stomach furiously flutter and she blushed. She too, would prefer the real thing and silently thanked her mother for her meddling.

"What were you doing before I arrived?" he said, once they were sitting at the table and realised she had been shoving paper into her handbag.

Once again a blush crossed her face.

"I was actually looking at my map of America," she said.

His laughter made her cheeks go even redder.

"So while you're waiting for your blind date, you're trying to work out my sisters' names? That's not weird at all," he smiled.

"It was something to do and easy to carry, that's all," she said, defensive. He made it sound like she was cheating on her blind date. "Besides, since you're here, let me run a few places past you."

Silently he groaned, but he did enjoy teasing Jacqui and had to admire her tenacity at trying to solve his sisters' names. She might actually be the first person anyone in his family had ever met that actually solved them without just giving up and being told.

Looking at her, tonight seemed so different to the other times they had dinner. Admittedly the first night, they hadn't even known each other and the last time, it was afterwork. But tonight, tonight actually seemed like a date to Phoenix and then he cursed the fact once again he left the rose in the taxi. Jacqui was a woman who deserved flowers and more.

The tie on her dress made his fingers itch to undo it and see if it fell open like he suspected it would. What would he find underneath? Before he could imagine, her voice was breaking into his reverie.

"So since this seems to be taking forever, is it cheating if I break it down state by state to knock those ones out?" she said.

"I can't see why not, after all, you're the one doing the deducing," he said.

"Great," she smiled. "I'll name a State and you tell me if their name is in it. If it's not then I can cross it out."

"Sounds good," he said.

"Hawaii?" shc said.

"No."

"California?"

"No."

She started on the west coast and was finding herself becoming more and more glad that she had decided to do it this way otherwise she really would have been at this forever. As she progressed, large chunks of the country were being crossed off until she was almost two-thirds done.

"I swear, if you say their names are in Maine, I'll kick you," she sighed, frustrated.

"Phew, my shins are safe," he grinned.

"Florida?"

"No."

Now she was jumping around. She needed to stick to her plan otherwise she'll probably end up getting it last when it could have been next if she hadn't changed her logic.

"Are they in the same State?" she said.

"No," he said.

"Okay, so at least there's two out of the few left. That makes me feel better," she said.

"Does it?" he grinned, making her want to kick him in the shins.

"My nemesis State, Virginia?" she giggled.

"Bingo," he smiled.

"Hallelujah," she said, relieved. "One down and one to go. Atlanta?"

"No, and it's not a State," he grinned.

"You know what I mean," she huffed.

"No, I don't," he said, facetious.

"I meant Georgia, I just got mixed up, that's all," she

scowled.

He thought she looked so cute when she was frustrated and running out of steam. Luckily, she finally got the last one.

"Bingo and there you go, you've won," he said.

She looked at him with her wide hazel eyes in disbelief and he felt that punch to his stomach again.

"I got them? I truly got them? *Finally*. My brain is fried," she groaned.

"Well you got the States their cities are in," he said, feeling bad for sort of ruining her little victory. "I'm sure a little dessert will cheer you up. Something to celebrate your victory."

She eyed him wondering if he knew her weakness was desserts, but didn't care. She did deserve something decadent.

"How's work going?" she said.

He groaned not wanting to talk about work but still, it was something to break the silence that seemed to have fallen over the table.

"Great. You?" he said.

"Busy," she said.

"Have you lived in New York all your life?" he said, changing the subject.

"Pretty much. We lived in New Jersey when I was really young and then when the company really started taking off, we moved to New York because my father wanted to be closer to work," she said. "What's it like living in New Zealand? I have to admit, as you know, I know nothing about it."

"You mean you didn't google it after our first blind date?" he teased.

"No. I don't really google people or places like lots of people do these days, which of course you could say is stupid, but I'd like to think getting to know someone from what they tell you is better than researching them. Of course, if you were a con artist then I'd feel like a prize idiot for not doing it," she said.

"No, I get it. The power of the internet is great, but if you have to google someone then is that really getting to know them or is it just being lazy?" he said.

"What do you mean by that?" she said.

"Well, let's say you googled me and found I'm really a janitor at the company or not the CEO as I lead you to believe. Does that mean you ghost me or do you think to ask me to clarify what you found the next time we meet, if we meet?" he said.

"Oh I see, have I already judged you by what I found if it doesn't fit into what I think of you," she said.

"Yes. I've had dates who have unbeknownst to me, googled me in the bathroom and then come out and say that I'm not high enough on the ladder for them to bother about. It doesn't matter I'm working my way up or that I have a good job. They want the CEO only," he said, trying hard to not sound annoyed.

"Then you're better off without them. A relationship with them would never have lasted since it's not actually you they want, but the superficial or materialistic stuff," she said.

"Exactly," he said, happy Jacqui could see his point of

view. "So apart from the drug dealer, the wannabe gang-banger and the two-timer you mention on our first date, what other losers have you had lucky escapes from?"

"You remember that?" she said, surprised and also happy he remembered.

"Kind of hard not to, since it's not every day someone confesses to have dated a drug dealer. Well, anyone I know of anyway," he chuckled.

"The two-timing accountant was so pedantic about money he would calculate the tip down to the last penny. You know that saying: not a penny more, not a penny less, that was him. Although admittedly, he was a lot more flexible about it being a penny less," she smiled.

Soon she had him laughing at some of her terrible boyfriends and dates and for the first time in ages, Jacqui actually found her love life, as disastrous as it was, something she could laugh at. But maybe that was because Phoenix was laughing with her, not at her or judging her bad choices.

"You can't tell me you've never had a terrible date or girlfriend," she said.

"Not really," he shrugged. "My sisters on the other hand have had some doozies. Let's see there was the time Indi wanted to impress some dork. Then there was the time she accidentally kissed the wrong guy."

His stories about his older sisters made her laugh and feel like she was just as normal as they had been.

"And look at them now, happily married with children," she smiled.

"Yes, but even that path to true love wasn't exactly smooth," he said.

"What do you mean?" she said, eager to hear more.

"Where do I start?" he sighed. "It's a long story, but perhaps I'll leave it for another day since, you've finished dessert and it's getting late."

As much as he didn't want the evening to end, he knew it was going to have to at some point and also didn't want to spend more time with Jacqui in a restaurant.

Reluctantly she agreed Phoenix was right. Dare she invite him back to her place or would he invite her back to his?

"Can my taxi drop you somewhere?" he said, praying she'd at least let him see her home, even if he only got a kiss goodnight.

"I'm that way," she pointed.

"So am I," he smiled.

"In that case, yes you can," she said.

Outside her apartment building, he walked her to the door.

"Well, goodnight and thank you for a lovely dinner, I'm sorry I forgot the rose," he said.

"You don't have to keep apologising for that, it's okay," she smiled. "I don't suppose you'd like to come up for a coffee?"

The words left her mouth unexpectedly and the surprise was written all over her face.

"Are you sure? I'm happy to leave," he said.

She inhaled a deep breath.

"Yes, I'd love for you to come up," she said.

His smile was wide and bright and once again those fluttering sensations in her stomach went into overdrive.

The air crackled between them as they silently rode the elevator and walked to her apartment.

Inside her apartment, Phoenix noted everything was tidy and very homey.

"Take a seat and make yourself at home. I can't wait to hear the story of your sister's courtship," she said, taking off her coat,

"Why don't I tell you in the morning over breakfast," he said.

"What do —"

Before she could even ask what he meant, his mouth was on hers and all thought was gone.

Chapter Ten

The next morning Jacqui woke up in Phoenix's arms and couldn't help but smile. The man was a sex god who made her more than satisfied. She was pretty sure she managed to make him more than satiated as well.

Sighing, the puff of air tickled his skin and he woke.

"Good morning," he grinned. "I hope you slept well."

"Better than well," she smiled. "You?"

"Same, although now that I'm awake…" He pulled her on top of him and kissed her before smoothly entering her.

"You're insatiable," she moaned, loving the feeling of Phoenix inside her.

"Only with you," he said.

"Oh yes, I like that," she said.

"It'll feel better for the both of us if you sat up more and rode me hard," he said.

"*Oh yes*," she moaned again, as his hands got busy while

she moved up and down.

He shifted a little and she realised he propped himself up with the pillows.

"Now lean forward a little," he said.

As soon as she did, his mouth soon found one breast and then the other. Her speed picked up and soon she was galloping as they both finished together.

"Now it's a great morning," he chuckled.

"I need a shower," she said.

"Can I join you?" he said.

She wanted to say no, but the sexy look of desire on his face ensured she could only say yes.

"I can't believe it, but I'm actually going to say I'm officially sexed out. I don't think that's ever happened to me before," she said, later when they were snuggled up on the couch together.

"I can't say that's ever happened to me either," he said.

"Really?" She raised her head to look him in the eye.

"Really." He kissed the tip of her nose.

"Well, since neither of us can move, how about you tell me that story about your sister," she said.

"It's long," he groaned.

"I've got all day," she smiled.

"Okay," he said. "Indi first met Jason when she was housesitting for her boss and needed to borrow some sugar because she accidentally spilt his."

Hearing Jacqui's gasps and giggles and sighs made it all worthwhile, he thought as he finished the story.

"That's like something out of a movie," she said, shaking

her head in disbelief.

"We all think so. I'm just glad it all worked out," he said.

"I can't believe that he won her in poker," she said, amazed.

"Technically he didn't, but we all just say he did because it sounds better," he laughed.

"Do you know when Charles met Cynthia it was all very proper? I mean, super duper proper," she said, as he looked nonplussed. "Cynthia likes to act like she some kind of blueblood and put on airs and graces. She also acted like she needed to adhere to all these proper rules, like the need for chaperones and the like. For the life of me I couldn't understand it, but Charles seemed to fall for it hook, line and sinker. I think he only kissed her and didn't get to sleep with her until they got married."

Phoenix couldn't help but laugh at the picture. There was no way he could do that if he found the woman he wanted to married.

"Like you said, they're happily married so clearly it worked out and she was the right one for him," he said.

"I hope so. I'm just worried if he does sell the company and they spend all the money, she'll just leave him high and dry because to me, she's very materialistic and cold. I truly don't get what he sees in her," she said, with a sad shake of her head. "Stupidly, I once thought after he married her, I would finally get the sister I was dying for. Turns out, she's more like a cold relation you really don't want to have to spend any time with."

He hugged her to him knowing if he married Jacqui, his

family would not only welcome her with open arms, but also be the siblings she longed for, whether she wanted them or not. They would constantly be all up in her business.

A sense of peace came across him at that thought. He never thought of any of his girlfriends in such a permanent way, couldn't even picture them like that and yet, with Jacqui it just seemed to come naturally.

What did it all mean?

After lunch it was a nervous Jacqui who knew now was the time to broach her idea with Phoenix. Would he be on board or think she was crazy? She wasn't sure she wanted to see his reaction, but she also needed to know his answer.

"Nix, you know how you said that you work in investment finance?" she said, hesitant.

Uh-oh, he thought, this was the moment he was dreading, Jacqui knew she was his boss. Damn, he should have said something earlier, but then he wouldn't have had a spectacular night with her and it was more than worth her anger at him.

"Uh-huh," he said.

"I have an idea I want to run past you. You see, if Charles is going to sell, what do you think of me trying to find a group of investors who will buy it and then I can run the company?" she said, anxious.

This was way worse than Jacqui just finding out she was his boss. Now she was asking for his help and he had already got the ball rolling with his family. Now what was he going to do?

"There's a few questions you have to ask or have answers

for," he said, feeling more comfortable if he treated this like any other investment opportunity.

"Shoot," she said.

"How much risk is there for everyone? How much money are you asking them to invest? How many investors? Who gets what say in the decisions? How much of your own money are you planning on investing or none at all?" he said.

Jacqui bit her lip, she hadn't thought about any of this stuff, probably because it would then make the whole thing a lot more real, and it did.

"I hate to say it, Jacs but I'm not sure even if you did manage to get a group together, that they'd allow you to run the business. They may want someone else?" he said, feeling horrible for stating the truth.

"What? Why? Who would this other person be? They don't know the company like I do. Besides I do everything now —"

"That's exactly my point. When do you tell them, if you tell them at all, that your own father won't let you run the company or alternatively, why isn't Charles selling to you? If he is and you're looking for investors to help you buy it, then you're going to have to prove you're taking some of the risk by putting your own money in. If you're only going to be using their money, they then get to make all the decisions and may not have the confidence in you running Aurora, but will be happy to keep you where you are," he said, hating to be the one to tell her the hard truths because it felt like he was kicking her when she was down.

Jacqui's head was aching at the scenarios Phoenix just

laid before her. In her mind it seemed so easy, whoever she managed to get to invest would want her to keep running it, since she was already so successful at it. Unfortunately, they also wouldn't know she was the real CEO and if she let the cat out of the bag, they may not believe her or think she was just being fantastical. To her dismay Phoenix's advice made sense. Maybe she just was never destined to run the family business.

Wanting to take Jacqui's mind off Aurora and to see her smile again, he distracted her by telling the story of how Boston and Alyssa met.

"Boston didn't realise men were using his name to score women. They even had fake business cards made up to make it seem more legitimate," he said, as she gasped in disbelief. "Alyssa was in an accident where she was knocked unconscious by a mugger running away from his victim and so Lys ended up in hospital. The nurse called Boston on the pretext he was Lyssa's boyfriend to let him know, but it was really Lyssa's Uncle Jack who bribed the nurse to do it. At that stage no one knew Lys had amnesia and so Jack's meddling seemed harmless. Let's just say Lys recovered her memory, thought Boston was an imposter of himself, dated the fake Boston thinking he was the real one before finding out the truth, and now Bos and Lys are happily married."

Once again, Jacqui couldn't believe her ears. She thought Indi's story was not only far-fetched and enough drama for Phoenix's family, but to have two drama-filled stories like something out of a movie, just didn't seem plausible.

"Are you sure you're not just making these stories up for

my benefit?" she said, sceptical.

"I swear, they're both true," he chuckled.

"Well, what about Montana. You haven't said what kind of movie drama she had with her husband," she said.

He wasn't too sure what to say as he didn't know whether to mention Montana had been widowed. It was a period of her life which was bleak and although James was mentioned on occasion, everyone knew she'd happily moved on with Lucas and was loving her life.

"Mon went and married the very first 'hunky Italian god', those are her words, we all just say the very first Italian man she ever met, or her first ever *fling* who just happened to be the very first Italian man she ever met," he chuckled. "She met Lucas when she was on holiday with her best friends and he was there with his cousins. His cousins and her best friends are now all married and living in Italy."

"So her best friends found Italian men as well, that's great," she said.

"That's the classic mistake everyone makes," he laughed. "No, Lucas' cousins, Marco and Tonio married Montana's best friends, Izzy and Toni."

The stunned look on her face made him laugh.

"So, Marco married Izzy? Or Toni?" she said, hesitant. "Please say Izzy because the idea of Tonio and Toni marrying is hilarious."

"You got it. Marco did marry Izzy and Tonio and Toni did get married," he grinned.

She couldn't stop laughing. People normally did get a kick out of the fact that Tonio and Toni, two people with such similar names, married.

Phoenix stayed the night again something he had never done before without it having been preplanned and left early the next morning so he could go home and change his clothes.

He left a very happy, sleepy and satiated Jacqui with a very thorough kiss goodbye and couldn't help smiling and whistling the entire way home.

He had just left his apartment when Tony rang sounding secretive and wanting to meet up, so Phoenix went to meet his friend instead of going to the office.

"Okay, what's with all the cloak and dagger? Don't tell me we're on the move again," he laughed, referring to all those years ago when Tony told him he was moving to New York.

"Not this time," Tony chuckled.

They were meeting in a café far away from the office and Tony had picked a table well away from any potential eavesdroppers.

The news Tony overheard blew his mind and he needed to tell someone before he exploded. Since he knew Phoenix could keep his mouth shut, his protégé was the perfect person to confess to.

"I overheard by complete accident, Charles Richmond talking to his wife about selling Aurora," he said. Phoenix's lack of reaction wasn't something Tony expected, which stunned him even more. "*You know?* How do you know?"

"Someone told me in confidence," Phoenix said, squirming.

"Who?" he said.

Knowing he was on the hot seat and knowing Tony was feeling a little betrayed Phoenix hadn't told him the news, he also knew if he told Tony the truth, then perhaps his mentor and friend could help him.

"Jacqui," he said.

"Jacqui? Jacqui," Tony said.

Seeing Tony's facial features constantly change as he said her name around and around trying to put a name to the face, made Phoenix want to laugh.

"Jacqui Richmond? Charles' sister?" Tony said, stunned.

"Yes, that Jacqui," he chuckled.

"How? When? Why?" Tony said, unable to even begin to comprehend how Phoenix not only knew Jacqui Richmond, but managed to have her tell him something so explosive.

"It's a long story…" he sighed.

"Oh, I've got tons of time for this," Tony grinned, and Phoenix relaxed.

"It was a blind date and I was her date's stand-in because he couldn't make it. Anyway, we got talking and she really needed to get that off her chest and so she told me," he said.

As predicted Tony was stunned by Phoenix's story.

"I was thinking perhaps I should give Boston a little wink, wink, nudge, nudge on the sly," Tony said.

When Phoenix remained silent, Tony knew Phoenix had already told his brother.

"So what did Boston say?" he said.

"Actually, I was trying to get them to buy it," Phoenix said, but didn't add *for me*. However, Tony was sharper than that and knew Phoenix too well.

"It would take time for you to get up to speed with such a large and complex company, but you could do it if you give it time and patience," Tony said.

Now it was Phoenix's turn to be surprised.

"You know I want to run it?" he said.

"It's pretty obvious, at least to me. You wouldn't let something like this just slip through your fingers. Boston was right when he told me years ago you were a numbers whiz. Like I've always said, you have what it takes to go far. But what about Jacqui?" Tony said.

"That's a whole other kettle of fish," he groaned. "She casually mentioned getting a consortium together to buy it, so she can run it."

"She wants to run the company?" Tony said, stunned.

"Well, she is Charles' executive assistant and Gene's daughter. It could be a good look for the new owner to have her in charge, sort of business as usual," he said.

Tony stroked his chin. He hadn't gotten to where he was today by being stupid.

"You know I always had this funny feeling about Charles. When we're in meetings or talking one on one he's always vague or tells me he'll check and get back to me. Then when he does, the answers were so thorough I always thought he just wasn't a guy who knew off the top of his head. Now I'm guessing my instinct is correct. Jacqui is really the brains of the operation, isn't she?" Tony said.

Now it was Phoenix's turn for his jaw to drop at Tony's deduction.

"I don't know," he said, truthful, the thought never occurred to him that was the case. "But I'm sure she'd be more than capable to run it."

"The fact Jacqui wants to get a group of investors together and then run it speaks volumes, maybe not to a lot of people, but to me, *volumes*," Tony smiled.

Tony's words made Phoenix wonder if his mentor was right. Was Jacqui really running the business, but then what was wrong with her brother? Although it could also explain his decision to sell.

"You won't say anything, right?" he said, anxious.

"No, her secret's safe with me. So about Boston buying the company, is it too late to also get in on the action?" Tony said.

"To be honest, I don't know what's happening on that front. I've left it in their capable hands. However, I still don't know what to do about Jacqui's idea. I've tried to give her impartial advice like I would to any client. Stuff I don't think she's actually thought of," he said. "I even warned her even if she did succeed, her group of investors may not want her in the top job."

"How did she take that?" Tony said, totally agreeing with Phoenix. He had done the right thing.

"Not well. She couldn't understand why they wouldn't if she put the group together. So I spelt out a few other not so nice scenarios which could happen and I think I crushed her hopes," he said.

Seeing Phoenix look so dejected made Tony wonder if his friend actually had feelings for Jacqui Richmond.

"So you add her to your group of buyers," Tony said.

"I can't. What if she tells them she wants to run it? Even if I back her, it's not my money and I don't get a say. No matter which way this ends up, it's going to be bad for her. I don't think she's ever going to get her dream of officially running the company," he said.

"You like her a lot, don't you?" Tony said.

Before this weekend he would have brushed Tony's question off with a casual "of course", but now after spending so much time with her he couldn't deny it.

"Yes, I really do," he said, his face solemn.

"I don't know how you managed to get yourself into this pickle, but I'm sure it'll all work out," Tony said, trying to be supportive. "So she doesn't know you've told Boston on the sly?"

"No, it happened after I just met her and before, well, you know," he said.

"Before you liked her so much that now you're caught between a rock and a hard place," Tony said.

"That pretty much sums it up," he said.

"How about this? I call Boston, let him know what I overheard, ask him to cut me in on the action and that way, should Jacqui find out your brother's buying Aurora, you can tell her it was me who told him," Tony said, feeling sorry for his friend. This wasn't a situation he'd like to be in the thick of.

"I can't let you do that," he said. "No, if Jacqui finds out, I'll take responsibility since it is my fault."

"Then tell her," Tony said.

"What?" he said, surprised.

"Tell her you blabbed to Boston," Tony said.

"But then she'll have all this hope she'll be in charge," he said, confused by Tony's advice.

"No, you tell her the truth," Tony said. "That probably no matter who buys the company, she won't be put in charge. It'll hurt like hell, but she can never say you haven't been honest from the get-go."

"But I haven't been," he said, miserable.

"No, you idiot. I meant about her being in charge. If you keep trying to walk this tightrope, you're going to fall off without a safety net. If you want to keep the company and the girl, you're going to have to do that hideously, unsupportive and *honest* thing and tell her that to her face. She might hate you in the short term, but in the long run, hopefully she'll see you were right and forgive you," Tony said.

"I don't know… I mean, I haven't even told her I work for Aurora," he said.

"What?" Tony said, gobsmacked. He hadn't seen that coming at all. "She doesn't know?"

"No, I never told her and then when she told me about Charles and that she worked at Aurora, I realised she was technically my boss. I didn't want her to feel embarrassed or guilty for spilling her guts to an employee, so I didn't tell her," he said.

"And the last time you saw her?" Tony said.

"I still chickened out. As soon as I tell her, I'll be fired for sure," he said.

"Jeez, I've got to hand it to you, Nix. You know how to make sure your life is up the creek without a paddle and with a gigantic hole in the boat," Tony said, still trying to process all he learned. "You have to confess *it all*. It's not fair to Jacqui or yourself."

"God, I hate it when you're right, and hate it even more you've just said what my entire family would have also said. Bah, who needs all you know-it-alls in my life. Where are the people telling me to not tell, that she won't find out, that I'm not hurting anyone," he moaned.

"Let's just say we're all too honest for our own good," Tony laughed. It was a compliment to be compared with Phoenix's family.

Thanks to Tony, Phoenix now knew he needed to tell his family. It wasn't something he wanted to do over the phone and so he arranged to fly over on Friday.

Chapter Eleven

"Lucas couldn't be here without making Mon suspicious, especially if she finds out you're here again as well, so he's dialling in and we'll put him on screen," Boston said.

"What about Indi and Lys?" Phoenix said, nervous. Trying to sneak around his family was practically an impossibility since they talked all the time.

"Jase is going to say he's at golf and Lys promised not to say anything but let's face it, she's not a great liar so if the states ask, she'll spill the beans like a burst dam. Hopefully it will be well after you're gone and this is all sorted," Boston said.

"Thanks Bos, but I'm still kind of nervous," he said.

"Why?" Boston said.

"Wait until we get started," he said.

From the look on his brother's face, Boston already knew what Phoenix was about to tell them. He had fallen in love with Jacqui and they were either to call it all off or he was going to tell her the truth.

Unbeknownst to Phoenix, the three men already discussed this possibility and made plans. They wanted Phoenix to get the girl and the company.

Phoenix also didn't know someone had made contact with Charles and his wife in a seemingly random meeting in which it seemed Charles' wife was quite happy to tell their contact Charles was selling. That meant the news was sure to break very soon. Luckily thanks to Phoenix's forewarning, they had already managed to sort out how they were going to buy Aurora and approach Charles with an offer he couldn't refuse, while others scrambled to get an offer together. Hopefully by then it would be too late.

In trying to protect his brother and save any kind of relationship he might be able to salvage with the woman they all thought would be his future wife, they purposely left Phoenix out of the loop, giving him no updates.

Unfortunately for them, knowing Phoenix's quick temper, they could all be in for a pounding, except Lucas who couldn't be there in person. Lucky dog, Boston thought to himself.

Boston had also been forewarned by Tony, who wanted in on their group. Putting Tony's name into the hat, Jason and Lucas both agreed since he had been good to Phoenix all these years.

"We're willing to give you one percent," Boston chuckled, when Tony called.

"One percent," Tony huffed, feigning indignation. "After

all I've done for you, all I get is a measly *one* percent. Well, that's gratitude for you."

"Fine," he sighed. "We'll each give you one percent of our share, that's four in total."

"With friends like you, who needs enemies," Tony said, but knew this was Boston's way of thanking him and they appreciated all he had done. "After all the years I've had to put up with Nix, training him and taking him with me around the world, I only get a measly *four* percent. Make it five and I won't charge you fees on your business anymore."

"No, you won't but Nix would," he said, as they both laughed. "Fine, you drive a hard bargain. We'll let you have five at no risk to yourself, I might add, so don't push your luck."

"Huh? Now I'm confused. What are you talking about?" Tony said.

"We, out of the generosity of our own hearts *and wallets*, decided you *might* deserve some recognition for being such a great mentor to Nix all these years and so we'd like to *gift* you five percent, should we be successful and not a percent more," Boston teased.

Tony was stunned by their generosity. He honestly meant to invest with them.

"I-I don't know what to say? I mean, I'm happy to invest my money in the group too," Tony said.

"No, we decided it was just too much hassle and let's face it, your piddly little amount wouldn't even cover the bank fees of sending the money over to us. You can buy us all lunch or dinner the next time we're in town," he said.

"I-I'm stunned. Thank you seems so inadequate. And of course, lunch or dinner or both is on me. Only, can you come one at a time, I don't know if I can justify putting you all on the company card at once," Tony laughed.

"I knew it. You're such a cheapskate, you probably were counting on us being generous and waiving your investment," he said.

"Hey, I didn't get to where I am today by being an idiot. But seriously, thank you. Maybe now I can afford a family trip back to Europe," Tony chuckled.

"Don't forget to stop by and visit. Seriously, thanks for everything you've done for Nix, I know he appreciates it as much as we do. And it's true, you earned this. Nix is a pain in the arse," he said.

Jason arrived and then they got down to business once Lucas dialled in and was on the screen.

"Okay Nix, the floor's yours," Boston said.

Nervously, Phoenix wrung his hands knowing what he was about to say could end in arguments and recriminations or a fight and with his brother and brothers-in-law refusing to ever entertain going into business with him again.

Maybe he should start with the easy stuff first.

"So Tony overheard Charles talking about selling so I'm guessing the cat will out of that bag very shortly. He said he wanted in and would call you, Bos," he said.

"Done and sorted," Boston said.

"Huh? That was quick," he said, still trying to comprehend his brother's answer.

"Don't worry about it," Boston smiled, waving his hand.

"Moving on."

Now his nerves ramped up over what he was about to say.

"Well, one of the reasons I've come this time is because Jacqui asked me to find her a group of investors to buy the company and let her run it," he said.

"So you haven't told her we know," Lucas frowned.

"No," he said.

"And does she realise that just because she gets a group together they might not let her run the company either?" Boston said, wanting to be sure Phoenix hadn't given Jacqui any kind of false hope.

"Yes. I advised her in an impartial and general way, all the pitfalls that could happen," he said.

"How did she take it?" Lucas said.

"Not well. I don't think she thought about it that much in-depth. It's hard to know that whatever she hopes, her dreams are probably going to be crushed and she'll never have her name as CEO," he said.

He really didn't want to be the one doing the crushing, yet could see he probably would be.

"Have you told her she's your boss yet?" Jason said, concerned.

All eyes were glued to him and he felt himself begin to sweat.

"No," he said.

"Why haven't you told her?" Boston said, incredulous. "You're only going to make it worse when she finds out."

"Remember that pickle that you were never going to find yourself in?" Lucas said, referring to Phoenix's past remarks when Boston was dating Alyssa.

"Don't remind me," he groaned, as the others just smiled.

"Yes, it's happening and about to become worse a lot sooner rather than later," Lucas said.

It was the tone that caught Phoenix's attention.

"What does that mean?" he said, worried.

"It means Charles' wife is quite happy to tell anyone he wants to sell, which means we've had to up our up our timetable and present our offer asap," Boston said.

"When?" he said.

"Monday," Boston said.

"Monday!" he gasped.

"We don't have a choice. We need to get in first and have him sign on the dotted line before anyone else manages to either pool their resources or convince him to hold off," Jason said.

The nightmare that was about to become his life was about to occur only a few days from now.

"Is there no chance you guys would let Jacqui run the company?" He held onto a flicker of hope, which was immediately extinguished.

"I'm sorry, Nix but if you want to run it in the future, she can't because she'll end up resenting you and we'll end up with a big, fat, employment dispute on our hands," Lucas said.

"So who have you found to run it? It's not Tony?" He could feel his anger welling up inside him at the possibility his mentor and friend had done the dirty on him and installed himself in the top job.

"No, it's not Tony," Lucas said, as Phoenix breathed a sigh of relief. "As we previously said, we wanted someone with the experience who could train you up without making it look too obvious. Trevor Sacks is going to run the company for us."

Phoenix's eyes boggled at the name. Trevor Sacks was a legend in finance circles and Phoenix couldn't even begin to know how they managed to get the man not only out of retirement, but to also train him. Learning from someone like Trevor would be invaluable. It would also ensure Aurora's big clients would be more comfortable staying with the company knowing someone like Trevor was at the helm.

As excited as Phoenix was, he then realised Jacqui was going to be destroyed by the news and was never going to speak to him again. The thought weighed heavily on his mind.

"I know you're worried about Jacqui, Nix," Boston quietly said. "You really need to tell her the truth and soon, otherwise she'll never forgive you."

"That's what Tony said," he said, glum.

"We're sorry, Nix. None of us wanted you to be in this position," Lucas said.

"If you want, we'll call the whole thing off and let the chips fall where they may," Boston said, trying to give his brother options. Phoenix's happiness was more important than a company.

"We all agree, Nix," Jason said. "Just say the word and we won't approach Charles at all."

He shook his head, knowing his family were letting him

decide, but as an opportunity this was too good to pass up.

"No, this kind of opportunity won't come around again. I guess I'll just have to cross my fingers and hope like crazy that Jacqui will at least see we're the best of the worst case scenario for her," he said.

"We'll leave your name out of it when we're dealing with Charles so it could buy you some time with Jacqui, but once it's out we've bought it and you're related to us, the genie can't be put back in the bottle," Jason said.

"I know and I appreciate it," he said, raking a hand through his hair. "I didn't think this was going to be so difficult when I first mentioned it."

"That's because you hadn't truly fallen in love with her then. Now you have and your world is tipped off its axis," Boston said.

"Don't forget, we've got your back. Whatever you need from us, we'll help," Lucas said.

"So will the rest of our families," Jason said.

Once again, Nix was overwhelmed with the love and support he had from his family. There truly was no one else he could imagine having as great a family as his.

His original plan had been to spend the weekend in London with his family, but since they all seemed to be busy, he decided to return to New York and as he sat on the plane he thought about everyone's honest words. Shifting in his seat it was depressing knowing he not only had to be the bearer of bad news, but news which was going to completely crush

Jacqui. The thought of hurting her, made his heart ache and he wasn't sure what he could do about it.

In some respects, all of this was inevitable and it just came down to who was going to be the one who did it, and so he wanted it to be him. If she had to have bad news, it should come from him. Hopefully he could soften the blow even if it was only a little.

While everyone was right in saying Jacqui couldn't be the new CEO, if only they could see just how much it meant to her, for her to be taken seriously.

Thinking about Jacqui and her long brunette hair and vivid hazel eyes almost made him call her. Several times he reached for the phone wanting to hear her voice, but he always seemed to chicken out.

No, he'd wait until he saw her before confessing who exactly he was related too and what he had done. Just the thought of knowing in all fairness she was going to be beyond shocked and explosively angry at him, not to mention she was bound to accuse him of all sorts of betrayal, made his heart hurt like it was being squeezed in a vice.

Trying to put off the moment for as long as possible, even though time was quickly ticking by, Phoenix decided to visit Cameron.

"How was your trip?" Cameron said.

"Not bad. Not great either to be honest…"

Jen walked into the hallway and smiled seeing Phoenix.

"Nix, what brings you by? In fact, nope I don't even care. What I do care about is, how was the blind date?" she said, eager for an update.

Silently he groaned having completely forgotten he hadn't seen his friends since then and as much as he didn't really want to talk about it, he was glad for the distraction at the moment.

"Great," he smiled.

Jen beamed at his response.

"In fact, we had actually already met on a previous blind date," he said.

"Huh?" she said, confused.

He explained his role as stand-in at Jacqui's first blind date with Eddie.

"It seems Mabel and Jacqui's mother are good friends," he chuckled.

"That's hilarious," Jen laughed. "Well, at least it wouldn't have been an awkward date since you both knew each other."

"No, it was great. Two blind dates and they were both her. What are the odds?" he said.

Knowing Phoenix wanted to talk to him in private and needing a subtle way to get them alone, Cameron ended the conversation.

"Come on, Stan hasn't seen you yet, and you know he's always got a smile for Uncle Nix," he said.

"That's because Stan's smart enough to know by now I always come with presents," Phoenix chuckled.

"You spoil him," Jen happily chided.

"Hey, I'm okay with bribery," he grinned.

Stan was playing on the lounge floor and Phoenix offered him a tiny wooden red double-decker bus he bought. Stan giggled and promptly put it in his mouth, before throwing it.

"It's like watching Godzilla," he chuckled, as Jen took Stan away so the men could relax and watch some sport.

They sat in silence sipping their beers watching the TV screen flashing up numerous images.

Jen came back into the lounge with a happy Stan still holding his new wooden bus.

"Your turn to put him to bed. Give Uncle Nix a kiss goodnight," she said, giving Stan to Phoenix for a hug and a kiss before he was then duly passed over to his father.

Phoenix followed Jen into the kitchen.

"Can I help with anything?" he said.

"No. Just sit and tell me all about London. It sounds silly, but it would be nice to have a holiday anywhere," she sighed.

Phoenix knew she wouldn't trade Stan for anything especially a holiday. Watching Jen only set two plates, he was confused.

"Are you not joining us?" he said.

He didn't want to seem relieved at the possibility that she might be going out, but he was.

"Actually I've got dinner with friends so you coming over tonight was a godsend, because otherwise I'd be feeling guilty Cam would have been bored here all by himself," she said.

He chuckled knowing his best friend would have enjoyed the solitude watching all the uninterrupted sport he could.

They made small chit-chat over dinner until Jen left and then they got down to having a serious discussion.

"So what's going on? Last text was that you were zooming across to London," Cameron said.

"The genie is out of the bottle. Tony told me he overheard Charles was thinking about selling. You should have seen his face when he told me and I had to admit to not only knowing all about it, but from who," he said.

"Well, if only Tony knows, that shouldn't be too bad," Cameron said.

"It seems my family also sent out feelers and Charles' wife is telling everyone he wants to sell, so it'll be big news very shortly," he said, shaking his head.

"So what's your family going to do?" Cameron said.

"Get in quick and hopefully have Charles sign on the dotted line. They're approaching him Monday," he said.

"Oh wow. Did they tell you who they want to run the company and be your mentor?" Cameron said, curious.

Phoenix couldn't wait to see Cameron's face when he told him.

"Trevor Sacks," he said.

Yes, just like he pictured, Cameron's face was a cartoon character with bulging eyes and jaw falling to the floor.

"You're kidding," Cameron said.

"No," he smiled.

"Damn, I'm jealous. Think I can get a job there and learn from him too?" Cameron said.

"You wish," he laughed. "It's pretty exciting, the man is a finance genius."

"I know. I can't believe how lucky you are," Cameron said.

"Neither can I," he said.

"So what about Jacqui?" Cameron said, worried for his friend.

"Which reminds me, did you know Jacqui was my blind date when you set me up?" he said.

"Of course," Cameron smiled.

"You're lucky you're not only my best friend, but I'm not pounding you into the ground over your little trick. You could have told me," he huffed.

"I thought you'd like the surprise and besides, it was fun to think of you being really nervous until you realised who your date was," Cameron laughed.

"You wait, payback's a bitch," he smiled.

"Thankfully, I'm happily married. Now back to the topic at hand," Cameron said.

Phoenix had filled Cameron in on Charles and Jacqui's set-up and their dates earlier.

"That's the down side." He heaved a loud sigh. "How do I break the news to her that not only is there going to be an offer on the table but no matter what, she's not going to be running the company?"

It was the question he asked everyone and no one seemed to have any kind of answer for him.

"That's tough, man, I don't envy you. On the plus side, no matter who it is, no one would take the news well. Unfortunately, you get to be the bearer of very bad news and it will seem personal because she knows you," Cameron said.

"Want to do it for me? I'll get you a job and you can have some one on one training with Trevor too," he said.

"Tempting, very tempting, but alas I am way too chicken.

Sorry dude, you're on your own," Cameron said, sympathetic.

"I want my bus back," he pouted.

"Sure, if you can pry it out of Stan's hand. I think he's even sleeping with it, so don't be surprised if he wakes shrieking and then Jen will find out and kick your butt," Cameron grinned.

"I can take her," he said, full of bravado.

"Yes, you can but then there'll be no more free tickets to any games," Cameron said.

"Whoa, whoa, whoa, there's no need for that kind of talk. I was just joking," he said.

They both laughed and went back to watching TV.

Although it was nice to catch up with his friend, he still felt alone as he returned to his apartment and before he even realised what he was doing, he was knocking on a dark wooden door.

Chapter Twelve

Jacqui opened her door surprised to see the man on the other side.

"Phoenix! What are you doing here? I thought you were in London all weekend," she said, ecstatic.

As disappointed as she had been that he was seeing his family, she hadn't expected to see him. Now he was standing here in front of her, a flood of desire washed over her.

Just seeing Jacqui made his heart sing and relief swamped him that she hadn't been out on a date with another man. He didn't answer, just entered cupping her face and claiming her mouth like a dying man needing water. The door slammed shut behind him as they both helped him shrug out of his clothes, eager to be naked together, skin touching skin with nothing in between.

His mouth was hot on her skin as it moved from her mouth to her neck and back. His hands untied her silk robe and she didn't even notice it fluttering to the floor as all her attention was on his warm hard body and deliciously soft lips.

Somehow they found her bed and his mouth covered one bountiful breast, as she automatically spread her legs to let his hand have access to intimately tease her.

She arched against him eliciting a moan of pleasure as her hands slid across his shoulder blades to hold him even closer to her while her hips kept lifting revelling in having his fingers inside her even though she wanted him more.

He played her like a violin, sliding his fingers over her hard little nub, then inserting them in and out in a gentle moderate tempo.

"Please Phoenix," she said, her whole body on fire.

He didn't answer, he just moved to suckle her other breast, which set the fuse alight and sprinted straight to her very core.

"Oh God, more… Faster… Faster… Yes," she moaned, succumbing to the pleasure erupting inside her.

Panting, she collapsed back into the bed, limp and yet, he still hadn't finished teasing her. His mouth moved south to find his fingers and drink from her. Licking and lapping at her, her fingers bunched the bedding.

"Oh God, I need you so bad," she moaned, pleading for him to end the teasing and give her the one thing she truly wanted. Him inside her.

He reared up and she felt the shadow of him looming over her. Opening her eyes, they immediately widened as he plunged into her making her shout his name. His eyes were sparkling and she couldn't do anything, but look at his beautiful face filled with desire.

He was panting, his desire raging, yet he refused to give in to his own satisfaction until she came again. Having her look deep into his eyes as he moved fluidly in and out of her made him feel so much more connected, and he wasn't going to be able to hold on much longer.

"Phoenix!" she said, as he thrust hard once, twice, three times, climaxing before collapsing on top of her.

Both of them were too tired to move as she wrapped her arms around him and held him close. He could hear his heart beating and somehow in the calm all he wanted to do was hold onto this moment for ever.

That's when he knew everyone was right. He was totally in love with Jacqui. Closing his eyes, he slept.

After a morning spent in bed, they managed to get up and have some lunch.

"I thought you said you'd be in London all weekend," she said, delighted he'd surprised her. "You're lucky I wasn't out on a date or brought someone back here."

His scowl made her giggle.

"I wanted to see you," he said.

She blushed, feeling that fluttering sensation at his words. She didn't even care if they were the truth or not. Having Phoenix with her just made her happy.

Now that he had acknowledged he loved Jacqui, he leant over and kissed her. Knowing he needed to tell her the truth, the whole truth, while wanting to memorise everything he could about her before she angrily slammed the door in his face.

He remembered back to when Boston had been lying to Alyssa and how everyone had told him to tell her the truth, but his brother couldn't do it. Seeing the state Boston had been in after Alyssa found out and not from Boston, was the reason Phoenix knew he had to tell Jacqui. Learning from his brother's mistake, Phoenix could only hope and pray Jacqui would understand.

Reluctantly pulling away before they ended up removing their clothes once again. He saw the look of surprise on her face and could feel the heavy weight and anxiety of his confession hanging over his head.

"There's something I need to tell you. Something I should have told you right from the beginning," he said.

The serious look on Phoenix's face had Jacqui in a quiet panic. Did he have a girlfriend and been stringing her along? Even worse, was he married? Part of her didn't want to know and part of her knew, she had to know.

He decided to go with the easiest confession first.

"Technically, you're my boss," he said.

"Huh?" she said, confused. "I don't understand."

"When you told me you worked at Aurora, I should have told you then that I do too," he said, relieved she hadn't got mad *yet*.

"You do? Where? Since I've never seen you, it's not such a big deal," she said, relieved.

"I work in your investment division. Actually I'm now the manager under Nelson. Tony Santamaria brought me over from England with him," he said.

She remembered hearing some sort of kerfuffle about Tony bringing somebody with him, but that all died down.

"But you're not English," she said.

He wanted to laugh at her befuddled state, but couldn't.

"No, I'm not. You see, a lot of Kiwis go to England for their OE because they can live and work there. It's the gateway to Europe so it's a great place to base yourself and also travel," he said.

"I see," she said, but really she didn't. "Like I said, it's not a big deal since we don't see each other at work anyway."

"There's more," he said.

The silence in the room made the moment even more difficult to confess the worst of his news.

"I told my brother about Charles and asked if he'd look into buying the company," he said.

"That's great," she smiled, hope blooming in her chest Phoenix found a way for her to finally get Aurora. "Do you think he will? Will he let me run the company?"

"I don't think you understand. I wanted him to buy it *for me*," he said.

Jacqui staggered as if he had punched her in the face and that's exactly how it felt, only he was stabbing her right in the heart.

The look of realisation on her face was a million times worse than anything he imagined. His own heart was tightly squeezing, the ache hurting.

"Y-you want Aurora? You went behind my back after everything I told you…" She was speechless. Phoenix's betrayal was worse than anything her father or brother had ever done to her. “I can’t believe… This whole time, you’ve been using me.”

“That’s not true. You’re the one who brought it up. Not me. I saw an opportunity —”

“Just who is your brother anyway, that he has that kind of money. And I’m talking tens of millions of dollars,” she said, her voice so quiet he knew she was trying to process what he was saying while trying to keep the hurt at bay. “You’re taking my family’s legacy from me. I can’t believe this.” She shook her head, still reeling.

“Jacs, it’ll still be a family business, but it’ll be my family who owns it. I did try to get them to see you’d make a great CEO, but like I told you before, they want new blood,” he said.

“Them? Whose them? I thought it was just your brother?” she said.

“My family. My brother and brothers-in-law,” he said.

“I-I don’t know what to think. You conned me. You’ve been stringing me along all this time. Why? Why now? Why are you telling me this all now?” she said.

“Because they’re going to make an offer to Charles tomorrow. The word is out that he wants to sell,” he said.

“You’re lying,” she said.

Sadly he shook his head.

“But he said, he said he’d wait a year,” she said, the feeling of betrayal squeezing her heart so hard it hurt beyond anything she ever imagined.

The hurt in her voice, cut him deeper than anything he had ever known.

"Obviously he didn't want to wait that long," he said.

"So if this hadn't gotten out, then you would've just happily keep stringing me along to get more inside information." She gave a hollow, bitter laugh.

"It's not like that. From the moment we met, I've felt something I've never felt with any other woman," he said.

"Yeah, the potential to own a multi-million dollar company," she mocked.

Her insult hit its target so accurately he felt like he had been hit over the head with a frying pan.

"Get out! Get out and I don't ever want to see you again. You've had your fun and now you can leave," she said, furious, the tears pooling in her eyes.

"Jacs, *please*, I truly didn't do this to hurt you," he said.

"Well, it's a little too late for that," she said.

Beaten and resigned he did as she asked, knowing the look of betrayal in her eyes was something he was never going to forget.

As he walked, he wished he never asked his family to buy the company, but in truth, it would be a lie. The logical part of him, knew it was too good an opportunity to pass up. It was the fact he'd just lost Jacqui, and his own heart was breaking from his stupidity.

As soon as Phoenix left, Jacqui burst into tears unable to comprehend how she had just been suckered in and so well. She didn't know what hurt more, his duplicity or the fact she had somehow fallen in love with Phoenix without even realising it until he told her the ugly truth.

Her heart ached from missing him even though he had

only been gone a few minutes. Still it was there, a black and empty void.

Wiping her tears she decided to do the one thing she had never done. Perhaps if she had been smarter earlier on, she would have seen this coming, but in her own stupid naïveté she just foolishly trusted. Looking up Boston Chan on the internet, she found herself gobsmacked at what she found. There were quite a few articles on him and in all his pictures, she could see the family resemblance to Phoenix, which set her off crying again. As she trawled through a few of the articles, she found Phoenix and Boston's brothers-in-law were Jason Kwong Lee and Lucas Romero. She didn't recognise their names, but after searching for them, she was once again dumbstruck.

Phoenix was related to some very seriously wealthy people. Why had he never told her? No wonder he was so sure his family would be able to stump up whatever price Charles wanted. Now she was angry and so she picked up the phone to call Charles.

Charles smiled as he got off the phone with his sister even though she had just given him a thorough dressing down.

"What did Jacqui want, darling?" Cynthia said.

She didn't particularly like her sister-in-law, but since she was not only Charles' sister and executive assistant who managed to keep the office ticking over every time they went on holiday, which was frequently, then Cynthia put up with her. Besides, if Charles was happy to use his sister as his secretary, then Cynthia was happy as there was no chance of her husband having some ridiculous affair with the office help.

"To remind me I told dad I wouldn't sell the company for a year and she knew I was still thinking about selling," he said, gleefully rubbing his hands.

Cynthia gave a look of disgust. She couldn't believe her idiotic husband agreed to such a ridiculous thing, but that's what happens when she wasn't around to put a stop to such nonsense. Besides, Gene only knew because Jacqui tattled on Charles and at the end of the day, everyone knew Gene wouldn't listen to his daughter so Charles placating his father was the only option he had.

"Why does that make you so happy?" she said.

"Because she doesn't realise I'm meeting with Trevor Sacks tomorrow. *The* Trevor Sacks and he wants to buy the company. By tomorrow, it could all be done and dusted and we'll be free," he said, gleeful.

"Darling, you are just marvellous. We need to celebrate. Do I need to be there as well? I mean, I don't want to rain on your parade, but I want to ensure Trevor doesn't try to low-ball you. You know the man is devious and if he wants our company then it must be worth a pretty penny," she said, ecstatic. Soon this would be all over and they'd be drinking champagne and eating caviar in Europe with all the other rich and famous people.

"I'm sorry, darling, but if you're there I'm afraid he'll think that we're too eager or desperate to sell. I feel it would be better for it to be just us men. You know, two businessmen haggling. It could get ugly and I don't want you to see that side of me," he said.

"You're right as always, Charles. Although I'd like to feel a part of it," she said.

Seeing the disappointment on Cynthia's face, he knew she truly did want what was best for them.

"Well, what number do you think's too low and I'll make sure I won't accept anything less. That way, it'll be like you're there with me in spirit," he said.

He didn't want to tell her he had no idea just how much the company was really worth. He could get Jacqui to tell him, but knew she'd refuse since she was already angry at him for wanting to sell.

Admittedly, he did on the odd occasion feel a twinge of guilt over his sister. If she had been allowed to run the business, everyone would have been happy and none of this would ever have happened. Jacqui would never have wanted to sell, but alas, it wasn't the way it was. Now if only he'd actually paid attention to all those boring reports she made, then he wouldn't have to pluck a figure out of the sky.

"Twenty million should do nicely, but definitely more is better, darling." She smiled before leading him back to the bedroom. "Now, let's start the celebrations."

Chapter Thirteen

Trevor Sacks was a happily retired businessman. Although in truth it was probably more three quarters retired since Trevor still worked, but only on his own personal stuff. His children were running his company and any of the other businesses he hadn't sold off. Therefore it was a big surprise when Lucas Romero called to say he had a special interests project for him.

Trevor was one of those men who respected the younger man and on occasion provided him with some sound business advice.

"Trevor, I was wondering if you were up for a favour for me, all hush-hush of course," Lucas said.

"Since when is anything not hush-hush," he chuckled.

"This is super hush-hush," Lucas said.

"I'm intrigued. Tell me more," he said.

"You've heard of Aurora Financial Services?" Lucas said.

"Gene Richmond's company? Of course," he said.

"Well, I'm looking to buy it," Lucas said.

"I hadn't realised it was for sale," he said, surprised.

"That's why this is all hush-hush," Lucas said. "I've heard word Charles, Gene's son, is wanting to sell, but he hasn't made it public yet."

"So what does this have to do with me?" he said.

"I want you to act as my frontman, if you will, and buy it. I'm also wondering if you would perhaps also stay on as CEO and mentor Phoenix Chan to take over the reins of the company in due course," Lucas said.

"Phoenix Chan? Any relation to your wife?" he said.

Now Trevor was very curious. Lucas wasn't the kind of man to just buy a company on a whim for a family member and the fact he wanted Trevor to train up the future CEO was very telling. Clearly, Phoenix wasn't up to the job which begged the question, would he be any good at learning the ropes or would this company go be going down the gurgler in a few years. He wasn't quite sure how to tell Lucas, someone he respected, that this offer could be the end of a friendship. "Ah, I'm not sure —"

"My brothers-in-law and I don't want Phoenix taking over until he's ready, so it'll be on your say so. If you don't want the position, can you think of anyone else who might do it for us? We still want you to negotiate the buyout," Lucas said.

"Us? We? Now who are you talking about?" he said, bemused.

"Sorry Trevor, I thought it went without saying that Jason

Kwong Lee and Boston Chan are also involved in this deal," Lucas said.

"I should have realised," Trevor chuckled. Of course he knew of the men, and wondered if he was losing his edge if he hadn't really picked up they were all related until now. "May I ask just what Phoenix's business experience is like?" Silently he prayed the man had some sort of business nous going for him especially if Boston Chan was his brother.

"Of course. Nix is an investments wizard. Great with numbers. Is Tony Santamaria's protégé. He's just not experienced with managing a company, that's all. That's where you come in," Lucas said.

Trevor's head spun. He knew of Tony as well and that any protégé of Tony's had to be a whiz kid. Perhaps this job wouldn't be too bad unless Phoenix didn't have the head for management, which would be a shame.

"What if Phoenix doesn't have the head for management? You know not all people do," Trevor said, trying to be honest as he didn't want his own reputation to be sullied by saying yes, only to find out that men he knew and respected had blinkers on in respect to a family member. Trevor saw that kind of thing happen all the time.

"Tell us the truth. If we have to break it to Phoenix he's not CEO material then we will," Lucas said.

This was one of the things he respected about Lucas. The younger man knew not only where his talents lay but also others. He also wasn't one of those men who thought to put people into positions they weren't ready for.

He knew of many smart business people who would've

given the top job to undeserving people whether they were the right person or not, just for the simple fact of nepotism or that the people were very good friends.

Although Trevor was in the twilight of his working life, he loved a good challenge and after a flurry of discussions and thinking about it, Trevor agreed to do the job. He also knew this would make a lot of waves in the business community and he liked the thought of people speculating on just what he was up too.

However, he now frowned at the latest information he received on Aurora Financial Services. Obviously he knew Gene had built Aurora into a solid financial company and then one day just retired and handed it all over to his son, Charles. Lock, stock and barrel.

People were shocked by the move, however Gene said Charles could manage the company just as well, if not better than he, and Charles didn't need Gene looking over his shoulder all the time.

From the brief information Trevor received from some very deep sources, there was a rumour at one point that the son didn't inherit the father's intelligence for business, but since the company was still flourishing, the rumour died a natural death.

He also understood Gene's daughter, Jacqueline, who was a qualified accountant also worked there, but as Charles' PA which was a bit of a mystery in itself. If what he was told was true, then why wasn't she one of the senior executive team or even running the accounting division?

Arranging to meet Charles and put a ridiculous offer on

the table to see which way the wind blew, things quickly changed when Lucas told him time was not only of the essence if they wanted to get in first, he was to now put a serious offer to Charles.

Charles agreed to meet for a private lunch to discuss a possible buyout of Aurora.

"Charles, I'm so glad that you managed to find time in your busy schedule to fit me in," Trevor said, stroking Charles' ego.

"Of course, of course. After all, it's not every day that someone like you calls with a very tempting proposition," he laughed.

"Too true, and if things go well, I think that this lunch will be very successful," Trevor smiled.

"I agree," Charles said.

Over a lunch of polite chit-chat, Trevor began to realise Charles was either incredibly stupid or very good at playing dumb. Even basic knowledge about the company's financials or in general he didn't seem to know or have any grasp of, which led Trevor to wonder how the company had survived in business this long with him at the helm? Clearly he must have very capable senior executives. Then a thought occurred to him.

"It must be wonderful to have your sister working so closely with you in the family business," he said.

"Yes, Jacqui is definitely worth her weight in gold," Charles said.

"If you don't mind my asking, how come she's not a director of any of the departments or a part of the senior executive team?" he said.

Although he casually asked the question, Trevor could see Charles was beginning to squirm uncomfortably.

"She decided it really wasn't her thing at all and so I kindly offered to have her work for me so she could still be in the thick of things and a part of the family business. She enjoys the variety a lot more and still gets to use her accounting skills every now and then," he said.

Charles wasn't about to blab the truth or the fact that their father would never have given Jacqui such a placement in the company.

That's when the penny dropped. Trevor would bet all his wealth if he asked Jacqui the same questions he asked Charles, she would not only have the answers, but could rattle even more detail off the top of her head. This just made Charles wanting to sell and Jacqui not taking over as even more of a mystery.

"Well, you're very lucky to have such an extremely loyal sister," he said. "May I ask what your father thinks about selling? After all, don't we need his signature?"

The question might have been innocent enough, but it was enough for Charles to redden and bluster.

"For your information, my father gave me ownership of the company to do with it as I see fit. I find now is the right time to sell and he doesn't have any say at all," Charles said.

Seeing that the polite conversation was over and his curiosity satisfied that Charles didn't care about Gene's legacy, or whether his sister agreed with the sale, Trevor got down to brass tacks.

"So how much do you want for it?" he said, wondering if Charles was going to ask for the moon or give it away on a silver platter. To be honest, after all their talking, Trevor still had no idea how Charles' mind worked.

This was it, Charles gleefully thought. The moment was finally here and once they agreed on a price then he'd finally be free of the millstone around his neck. A millstone he never wanted. Once the company was sold there was nothing his father or sister could do. He'd be free.

Charles licked his lips knowing Cynthia wanted at least twenty million, but he wanted more. However, if he asked for too much, would Trevor laugh at him? He didn't want this company and wanted to be rid of it.

"How much do you think it's worth?" he said, torn between indecision.

Trevor tried hard not to look gobsmacked by Charles' question. It was one thing to ask someone when you own a company for curiosity's sake or planning for the future, however Trevor knew Charles was actually asking because he truly had no idea how much Aurora was worth.

Deciding to low-ball Charles and see what he said, Trevor also knew if he got this for a song, then Lucas Romero wasn't just in his debt, but had somehow managed to find the one owner in all the world who was an imbecile.

"Fifteen million," he said, offering a ridiculous price.

Charles was ecstatic, this was close to what Cynthia wanted. Now he was about to show his impressive negotiating skills.

"It seems a bit low," he frowned, after all he knew Trevor

had pots of money. "I was thinking more along the thirty million mark."

Trevor was pleasantly surprised, maybe Charles wasn't a complete idiot after all. Well, not when it came to money in his pocket. He tried to look deep in thought at the counter-offer and saw Charles start to sweat, which meant he thought he had pushed Trevor too far.

"I just don't think the company is worth that much," Trevor sighed. "I mean, there are rumours the company isn't doing so well, which is why you want to flick it off on the quiet before anyone finds out."

He was blatantly lying through his teeth and seeing the frightened look on Charles' face made him have to hide his smile. He truly hadn't had this much fun in years.

Charles was now panicking. Was what Trevor said true? Was the company not performing? Why hadn't Jacqui told him? Should he stall and ask Jacqui if it were true? But surely Trevor would know? He couldn't risk trying to sell a dead horse. He wanted to be free.

"Wh-what about twenty then?" he said, anxious. "Would that be okay?"

Charles wasn't even trying to play hardball and haggle over the offer, which is what Trevor, in all his years of being in business had never seen anyone do. Even someone who was on the brink of bankruptcy fought for more money harder than Charles.

Unable to hide his surprise Charles dropped his price so dramatically after one little fib, it now confirmed in Trevor's mind Lucas truly was a lucky s.o.b who had managed to find the world's stupidest business owner. As much as Trevor knew he could screw Charles down to his original offer, he knew that he and the men he represented didn't operate like that, especially since they were already getting the company for a song.

"Well, it is more than I thought I'd be paying," Trevor moaned, trying to make Charles feel better, but inside he was jumping for joy. "Fine, deal."

They shook hands.

"I'll get my team to start due diligence and the lawyers to draw up the necessary paperwork," Trevor said.

Once again Charles began to sweat.

"No, no, no need for that. As soon as I get the money in full, you can have the company," he said.

"But don't you want —"

"No. Just get the papers drawn up and I'll sign. I want this done asap before anyone gets wind of it," he said.

Trevor's mind boggled. Charles didn't show any interest into why Trevor wanted to buy Aurora nor any concern for the welfare of any of his employees' futures at the company. He also didn't attempt to haggle over any of the usual conditions most business owners did.

Charles, in effect agreed to sell his company for next to nothing with no strings at all, leaving Trevor to marvel once again at how Lucas managed to pick such a winner. Even if things at Aurora weren't great, the money he'd just saved purchasing it could bring it up to scratch in no time and there wasn't anything to stop Lucas from making any changes without repercussions.

"Sure, let me just get some details," Trevor said, still stunned by what had just happened.

The one thing Charles did request was that this was all to remain confidential until after the contracts were signed, which Trevor was more than happy to oblige. The last thing Trevor needed was someone else to learn of the deal and offer more money. The man sitting opposite him really was an idiot and Trevor wondered if Gene knew just how truly stupid his son was.

By the time Trevor got over his shock at what happened at lunch, he called Lucas over the internet knowing he couldn't wait to see the younger man's face.

"Trevor, how was the lunch? What happened?" Lucas said, eager to hear the news.

"I think you better get Jason and Boston on the line, they might want to hear this," he said. "Oh and perhaps a doctor and defibrillator as well. You're all about to have a heart attack." It was meant to have Lucas now thinking that it had all gone horribly pear-shaped.

"Okay, we're all here. How did it go?" Lucas said, anxious.

Trevor tried to smother his grin at hearing the worry in Lucas' voice.

"I'd like to say how I used my awesome and ferocious negotiating skills on your behalf, but that would be a complete lie. All I can say boys is that you three are the luckiest s.o.bs I've ever met," Trevor chuckled, seeing their faces.

"What do you mean? Did Charles actually sell to you?" Boston said, trying hard to not get his hopes up, but he was already celebrating to himself.

"Not only sold, but there's no conditions. Nothing. All he wants is his money and its done," Trevor said.

"No conditions? How on earth did you manage that?" Jason said, speechless. "It's unheard of."

"Like I said, it wasn't because of my savvy business negotiating genius, but because you boys are the luckiest s.o.bs around. Charles is worse than stupid. I threw him one little lie and he was sweating. Now I only wish I found him first," Trevor chuckled. "I do have to say it was the most fun I've had in years."

"So how much does he want?" Lucas said, concerned Trevor hadn't actually mentioned money yet.

"What was your limit again?" he said.

"Fifty mill," Lucas said.

"And how much did you think the company was worth?" he said.

"Thirty," Jason said.

"Thirty to forty," Boston said.

"Same," Lucas said.

"Am I allowed to keep the difference?" he said, and seeing their confusion, burst out laughing some more. "Boys I think you owe me for the big discount I managed to get you. In fact I want a mega pay rise now I know you can afford it."

"*Trevor*," Lucas growled, impatient.

"Hey, I'm enjoying myself. This is going to be one of my most favourite stories to tell from now on," he said.

"I'm guessing by the smile on your face you didn't need all our money so how much of it did you need?" Boston said.

"I started with an extremely low offer of fifteen," he said.

Jason whistled.

"He countered with thirty, which I have to say did surprise me. I didn't think he had the balls, and he didn't," Trevor said.

"*Trevor,*" Lucas growled.

"So I told him a little lie and suddenly his price plummeted to twenty," he chuckled.

"What?" All three men shouted their shock together making Trevor laugh as he saw their faces, it must have been similar to what he would have looked like if he had shown it.

"Are you kidding?" Boston said.

"He only wants twenty?" Lucas said.

"He is stupid," Jason said.

"I told him I'd get the lawyers to draw up the papers. He wants this done quickly and quietly," Trevor said.

"Let me just get the lawyers on it. No one is allowed to talk until I get back. I want to hear the whole story too," Jason said.

They agreed they would use Jason's lawyers for this purchase as they were the most experienced, but if Charles had no conditions then this would be the easiest money Duncan Dell & Partners would have ever earned.

Jason returned and then Trevor began his story. By the end of it, everyone was just as gobsmacked as Trevor.

"I can't believe it," Lucas said, amazed.

"Yes, and we're all in agreement with you that it wouldn't have been fair to screw Charles down even more, especially now that we know there's no conditions," Jason said, as everyone nodded.

"Like I said, I haven't had this much fun in years, I'm glad you thought of me," Trevor chuckled.

"Do you think this is why he wants to sell? He's in over his head and pretty soon the truth will start coming out that he's not a great leader or businessman since it's now been a few years since he's taken over the reins and can't hide it anymore?" Boston said.

"Possibly? Honestly if you were there, you'd know he couldn't even answer the most basic of questions. He definitely wants this sale done quickly. I don't think his father knows what he's up to," Trevor said.

"Oh, he knows," Lucas said, silently relieved Phoenix was right and hadn't been conned by a pretty face. "But apparently Charles said he'd wait a year before thinking of selling again, that's why we weren't in any rush and just lining up our ducks to get the jump on anyone else when the year was up. However, it seems Charles obviously wants out faster than anyone realised."

"Which is your good fortune," Trevor said.

"Well, I guess your retirement will be over very soon, you might want to take a vacation before the hard work starts," Lucas said.

"Are you going to keep the sister on?" Trevor said.

"That's a tough question. For now, yes, since she knows the ins and outs but after…" Jason said.

Trevor understood, it was always hard when new management comes in for employees to transfer their loyalty and what would Charles' sister do when he started using her as an executive assistant and wasn't running the show like he suspected she did now. It could make for interesting times ahead. Perhaps Lucas was right, it was time for a quick holiday.

Chapter Fourteen

Jacqui spent the rest of the weekend in constant tears and added to the lack of sleep, she had no idea how she had managed to roll out of bed this morning and make herself even slightly presentable for work.

She had rung Charles in a fit of rage to make sure he was still keeping his word about waiting for a year before selling the business. She didn't want to go into what Phoenix told her, but none of Charles' reassurances gave her any confidence. The only upside was the fact anyone who wanted to do due diligence or have any company information would have to go through her and she would therefore know if Charles broke his word.

Charles was in the office briefly this morning and then hadn't returned, not that it mattered since she didn't want to talk to him or let him see how upset she was over Phoenix.

That was another of her problems. Since he confessed to working in Aurora's investment department, she looked him up and burst into tears upon seeing his handsome face staring out at her. Luckily no one saw what a mess she was, otherwise they would have wondered what on earth was wrong with her.

Knowing she held the power to make the petty choice of firing him for no good reason, except lying, betraying and breaking her heart and yet, she still didn't have the heart to do it. She also didn't want to think of the possible employment grievance he could bring against the company especially if his family not only had very deep pockets, but were very close-knit. They would back him all the way.

Looking at the department's financials more in-depth in the hope of finding perhaps he wasn't pulling his weight and at his personnel record to see if she could find anything which could be of use to legitimately get rid of him, all she found was he wasn't just an exemplary employee, but was now the manager of Aurora's investment division as he said.

There was also the fact that since he had come on board the department's results were now the best they'd ever been, such was the dramatic and rapid change in fortunes. It seemed her father had been right to hire Tony Santamaria and Phoenix before he retired.

It made her want to throw something at her computer, she was that annoyed by Phoenix, even though he had no clue.

The rest of the week was much the same, she moped but was looking a lot more like herself. Charles, on the other hand seemed to be out of the office more and Jacqui was even beginning to suspect he was avoiding her. Still, since no one asked for any kind of company information, as the week went on, she breathed easier, slowly relaxing, knowing whatever offer Phoenix's family presented to Charles, her brother had kept his word and turned them down, for now at least.

She was envious of Phoenix and his large family knowing they would be all supporting him and surrounding him with their love, when she only had Charles and he definitely wasn't someone she could rely on nor confide in. That left only one other person, Alf.

"Hi Alf," she said, entering the butchery.

"Jacs, what can I do for you? I haven't seen you in weeks," he said.

He looked and sounded hesitant and she wasn't quite sure why until she remembered…

"Oh yes, big, fat, blabbermouth. I believe you just had to tell my mother not only about *all* my bad dates and boyfriends, but that you also set me up on a blind date," she scowled.

"Aw, come on Jacs, it wasn't like that. It just slipped out, that's all," Alf said, contrite.

"All my bad dates and boyfriends? All that information just *slipped out*? I think someone's trying to pull the wool over my eyes," she said.

"I swear it did slip out and then I saw the look in Fleur's eyes that she didn't know, so to cover it up I tried to tell her you managed to go on a blind date and met a really nice guy. I guess that just made it worse, huh?" he said.

Alf looked so apologetic and contrite she couldn't stay mad at him.

"It's okay, Alf. But for the record, thanks to your blabbermouth, my mother thought it would also be a great idea to set me up on a blind date," she said.

"Didn't you tell her you had the nice guy from mine on the hook?" he said.

Once again her heart ached. Alf's blind date seemed like a lifetime ago now, especially after all that had happened.

"Wasn't going to stop her so I had to agree to do it. She was feeling guilty my love life seemed like a trainwreck and was blaming it on my upbringing," she said.

"I see," he said.

She knew he would understand.

"So how was it?" he said.

"I don't think that you'd believe it. My mother and Mabel managed to set me up on a blind date with the same man who was the stand-in on your blind date," she said.

The stunned look on Alf's face made her laugh.

"You're joking," he said.

"No. Honest truth. What are the odds?" she said.

"So you're now dating?" he said. Seeing Alf's eager face made her even more miserable. This was where she had to break the news not only was she not dating Phoenix, but he was a lying scumbag.

"No," she said, miserable.

"What? Why?" he said, confused.

"Because we just didn't mesh very well," she lied, knowing the truth was they meshed all too well.

"I'm sorry, Jacs," he said.

"Me too."

Her phone pinged and as she looked at the message she was torn between laughing and crying. It was Edward wondering if she would like to try again for a date. Why now? Was it because he knew Phoenix and she were no longer any kind of item? A perverse sense of pleasure rolled through her. Perhaps Phoenix hadn't sent Edward her number because he liked her, until she remembered he had been only using her and if she dated Edward then Phoenix couldn't have dated or grilled her for his own nefarious purposes.

After texting Edward back that she would love to try again, she smiled at Alf.

"That was Edward asking me out on a date," she said.

"I guess my man is now in the running again," Alf beamed. "So what will it be for dinner?"

"I think chicken schnitzel, I feel like celebrating and this way I can have a yummy dessert," she said.

"That's my girl," he smiled.

Alf wrapped her order and she left feeling a little less miserable.

Jacqui was meeting Edward for dinner at Kanda and upon seeing him and his smiling face, it hit her at how handsome he was, so why would someone like him even need setting up in the first place?

"I really am sorry for leaving you in the lurch last time," he said.

"How is your sister and her baby?" she said.

"Actually its *babies*," he grinned, to her surprise. "That was the second shock after Nina was rushed into hospital to have an emergency caesarean, they found she was carrying twins."

"She didn't know?" she said, astonished.

"Believe me, we were all in shock not in the least Mike and Nina. Poor Mike had to rush out and buy an extra of everything," he chuckled. "Luckily, Nina and the twins stayed in hospital for a few days not only to recover, but to make sure the smaller twin was okay and gaining weight before they were sent home."

"Wow, I'm glad everyone's okay. So how's she coping with twins?" she said.

"It's been hectic, that's why I haven't had time to meet up with you. We've all been there helping them out," he said.

Once again, Jacqui was envious. This was the second guy she'd met who was close to his family. None of her exes were family orientated people, but wasn't that what she liked about them? They could do whatever they wanted, when they wanted, or was it because she hadn't exactly grown up in a close family, so she just attracted the same thing? It would also explain why none of those relationships ever worked out.

She hesitated to bring up the source of her misery and yet, found she couldn't help herself.

"So how do you know Phoenix?" she said.

"I met him through our mutual friend, Cam a few times. Actually it was Cam who told me about how Nix is a guy who's loyal and would always have your back. I knew if I told him the situation, he'd drop everything to help me out, even just to pass on a message," he smiled.

"He's definitely a good friend," she said.

Although clearly Phoenix hadn't told Edward he hadn't just passed on the message, he actually sat and dined with her, or the fact they were also set up on their own blind date. So was he really a good friend?

"Cam told me about this one time when Stan, his baby, was up crying and screaming with a high fever, and he and Jen were at their wits end so Cam rings Nix at midnight for support. Next thing he knew, Nix was at their place with a bag full of stuff he brought after ringing his sister in Europe for advice. His sister thought perhaps Stan might be teething, so he bought teething rings and some medicine to calm the fever. Jen had already given Stan medicine, and seeing his friends looking so frazzled and exhausted, Nix told them to go and get some sleep and he'd stay and comfort the crying Stan and give him some more medicine when it was due," he said. "Apparently after trying different positions, Nix realised Stan only liked being upright and once the teething rings had been in the fridge long enough to be cold, he tried it out on Stan who suddenly became an angel, happily chewing until he fell asleep. The next morning Jen and Cam found Nix asleep sitting in the armchair holding Stan."

She didn't need to hear great stories like that about Phoenix. All it did was dredge up horrible memories for her about how kind and nice he was. She remembered how outraged he was on her behalf when she told him her father wouldn't let her run the company, and the fact that he'd asked his family if she could run the company if they bought it. She didn't want to remember things like that. She needed to remember how he had used and betrayed her.

"So tell me about yourself," he said.

She told him that she worked for Aurora, but not that her brother wanted to sell. She'd learnt her lesson from the last time.

"Wow, talk about a close family. I don't think I could work that closely with Nina. She'd drive me nuts," he said.

Jacqui didn't have the heart to squash the happy image Eddie just portrayed.

"Being close to your family is great, isn't it? Nina having twins is a bonus since there's two babies to hold. My mother always commandeers one of the babies and if you even look to want to cuddle the one she has, she gives you one of her looks that has a million interpretations from 'how dare you take the baby from me' to 'don't you drop them'," he said.

Jacqui laughed. Wouldn't it be great to have a family like that, she thought.

"And while my mother might reluctantly give the baby to you, she then instantly commandeers the other one from someone or at any sign of movement or noise, she's quickly taking the baby back saying that thc baby needs her," he laughed.

After a great dinner, Jacqui realised if she had gone on the original blind date with Edward, she would have been happy to continue dating him. But now, all she saw was a great, funny guy. There was no chemistry other than friendship.

"Would you like to go out again sometime?" he said.

She hesitated unsure of what her answer should be.

"Can I ask you something first?" she said.

"Shoot," he said.

"I don't mean to be rude, but why did you need to be set up on a blind date? I mean, I know why I let Alf, my butcher of all people set me up, but why you?" she said.

He looked hesitant and thoughtful.

"I was in a relationship with my ex-girlfriend for four years and when we broke up I was devastated. Ever since then, I haven't really seriously dated. I mean, I had the odd date, but my heart just really wasn't into finding another partner until now," he said. "Wait. Alf's *your butcher*?"

The incredulous look on his face at her confession made her giggle.

"Didn't you know?" she said.

"No. My dad just told me Alf knew a pretty girl that I might like. He didn't say Alf's been screening his customers," he laughed. "Does he have some sort of questionnaire you have to answer every time you enter his shop?"

"No, only after the third visit and if you buy something. That way he can secretly judge by the cuts of meat you buy," she said.

They both laughed and then the mood turned sober as he waited for her to answer his question.

"I don't know how to answer," she said. "You see, if we had met on the original blind date, my answer without any hesitation would have been yes. But a lot of things have happened since then, and my life's a little complicated at the moment."

"Not that I wouldn't like to see you again, but I get it," he said. "Tell you what, if your life ever gets uncomplicated and you want to catch up, even as friends, give me a call," he said.

"Thanks, Edward," she said.

"Eddie," he smiled.

"Eddie," she smiled.

Jacqui left Eddie wondering if she had done the right thing. Surely going on another date with him wouldn't hurt. She fiddled with her phone wondering if she should text him and tell him another date would be great. Still her fingers didn't move and she realised perhaps she should just wait until this whole thing with Charles was over, whenever that might be. Then she could sort out her love life.

Perhaps Alf had been right all along, she just needed to find the shoe which fitted her, the only problem was, there were now two shoes who could possibly be her perfect match or *sole* mate. Groaning at her own pun, she headed home and went to bed.

Phoenix spent the first week after his confession not only moping and irritable, but waiting for the official *you're fired* letter from Jacqui. He knew she had every right to be petty enough to do it and wouldn't have blamed her. In fact, he probably would have just peacefully left knowing he could be back and be the one to turf her out on her backside one day.

There was one thing he could still do for her, even though it pained him, but for Jacqui he would. He sent Eddie her number, but no photo. He didn't want to sway his friend any more than necessary.

Although he asked Boston for an update on how the meeting went with Charles, his brother refused to divulge any information to him.

"Come on, Bos. Why won't you tell me?" he said.

"Because nothing's set in stone and until it's all done and dusted we don't want anyone else getting wind of this, not even by accident," Boston said.

"If you mean Jacqui, you don't have to worry about her anymore. I confessed and she threw me out," he said.

"Oh Nix, are you okay?" Boston said, sympathetic.

"Fine," he said, miserable.

"It hurts, doesn't it?"

"Like someone keeps stabbing me in the heart every time I breathe. Was it like this when you and Lys fought?" he said.

"That and a million times worse, especially since I knew she was the one for me. I didn't know how I was going to ever get her back," Boston said.

"Sounds right," he said.

"Listen I'm coming over —"

"Don't be stupid. It's not a big deal and I've got Cam to spill my guts too," he said, but really wanted his brother's support.

"True, but you also know family sticks together and when you hurt, we all hurt. Besides, I've got some business to tend to anyway. I'll be there tomorrow. Consider it good timing if you like," Boston said.

"I guess I'd better clean up the apartment and get rid of all the women then," he chuckled.

"If it's that bad, I want it sterilised from top to bottom too. Love you, bro," Boston said.

"Love you, too. And thanks," he said.

"That's what big brothers are for."

After Boston's call, Phoenix felt a sense of relief his brother was coming. It was true he didn't need him to rush over, yet it was nice to know they were still close and had each other's back. He would do the same for any of his siblings. He also knew whatever Boston saw or Phoenix told him would also be relayed back to the others unless he specifically said not to tell. Once again he shook his head knowing being part of such a large family was a blessing and a curse.

True to his word, Boston came to New York and Phoenix couldn't have been happier to see his brother. It was like old times, just hanging out and shooting the breeze.

"So how are you?" Boston said, noting the light in his brother's eyes had dimmed.

"Okay," he said, miserable.

Since it was only the two of them, he managed to tell Boston the whole story of what happened with Jacqui.

"Oh Nix, I'm sorry. We can still walk away. We'd rather

you have the girl than the company," Boston said.

"Thanks, I appreciate it, but you guys were right," he said. "It doesn't matter who owns it, they'll never let Jacqui run it. So the family might as well get the bargain of a lifetime out of it."

"Well, at least you've learnt from my mistakes and told her the truth, but it's still agony, isn't it?" Boston said.

"Don't I know it," he said.

Boston relayed the entire story of how Trevor bought the company, which was the real reason he was in New York.

"First and foremost was to see you and the other was to finalise the deal. Someone needed to be here to authorise the money with the bank," Boston said.

"I can't believe just how stupid Charles really is," Phoenix said, shaking his head.

"Neither can we to be honest, but we're not looking a gift horse in the mouth," Boston said.

"Jacs is going to have a heart attack when she finds out her brother basically gave away the company," he said.

"It's not her choice, nor does she have any say. If she did, we'd be paying through the nose, that's for sure," Boston said.

Boston's faith in Jacqui warmed Phoenix even though his brother had never met her.

"So when are you doing it?" he said.

"Tomorrow. I'm meeting Trevor and we'll discuss if I need to be there with Charles or if I should just stay in the background. After all, we don't want to scare Charles off," Boston said.

"Can Trevor sign the documents? After all, he's just a figurehead?" he said.

"No, so that's why we have to decide whether I come in just to sign and hand over the money or join the actual meeting from the start," Boston said.

"I think you should just waltz in, sign and then waltz out. It'll be a lot more impressive to Charles. If you sit in with him, he could start asking some awkward questions," he said.

"I highly doubt it, from what Trevor says," Boston chuckled.

"Hey, even an idiot can hit a bullseye every now and then," he grinned.

"Good point. I think I'll be too busy to do anything other than waltz in and out like you say," Boston said.

"Good to see that you listen to my advice," he said.

"Hey, I always listen, I just don't always take it," Boston grinned.

"Same here," he said.

Chapter Fifteen

Charles and Cynthia were ecstatic. Very soon they'd be free from the millstone hanging around their necks. She was also deliriously happy her husband managed to get twenty million for the company. Charles explained how Trevor tried to low-ball him with ten and then Charles showed just how savvy a businessman he was by managing to push Trevor to double his original offer. Even if she had known Charles was lying, she wouldn't have cared. All Cynthia cared about was that now they'd have pots of money to live their best lives.

Currently she was getting herself pampered so she could look her best for their celebration. Wait until she told her friends they were now mega-rich, they'd be so envious of her good fortune.

Later, she waltzed into Charles' office dressed as if she were someone of the highest importance, gave Jacqui a dismissive glance and breezed past her without a word of greeting, not caring whether her husband was busy or not.

Jacqui's face became pinched at Cynthia's unwanted presence. Her sister-in-law was another reason Charles was mismanaging the company since a lot of the company money was being spent on her. Cynthia was 'employed' by the company and spent up large sums of money on her company credit card. It was always for the same things, jewels, clothes and expensive luxury holidays, which Cynthia kept declaring she needed in order to portray the right image to the world about Aurora.

Unfortunately for Jacqui, it was always her who cleaned up Cynthia's spendthrift ways. Some of the excuses she made up to tell the company accountants were very vague and unbelievable and yet, everyone just seemed to understand that as long as someone signed off on it, a blind eye would be turned.

Briefly she wondered what any new owner would make of Cynthia's employment. If it was Jacqui, the first thing she would do would be to fire her sister-in-law and cut up her company credit card into thousands of little bits with an almost childishly petty glee, she wistfully thought.

Charles himself, had been deliriously happy when he came into work this morning. Having never seen him act like this in all the years she worked for him, her suspicions were on high alert as he usually he had a face like a man going to the guillotine. Something was definitely up.

"Jacqui, come in here, please," Charles said.

She took a few deep breaths to try and calm herself before she walked in pretending she was his happy sister.

"Yes, Charles?" She couldn't help but note both Charles and Cynthia were looking awfully smug with each other.

"I need you to go and get a well-chilled bottle of *the* most expensive champagne money can buy and have it ready for when we get back," he said.

"Oh, what are we celebrating?" she said, a horrible feeling of dread spreading through her. Surely Charles couldn't have sold the company so quickly. Every day an outsider didn't come sniffing around asking for information was a day she went home relieved. At this rate, the stress and agony of not knowing when the axe was about drop, would cause her to have a heart attack.

If she could just get Charles to tell her what was going on, then perhaps she might be able to put herself a few steps ahead of him, or at least give her time to adjust to the inevitable.

"We'll tell you when we get back," he said, as the glamour couple swept out of his office all aflutter. "Actually, forget that. Cynthia and I won't be back for the rest of the day."

A sinking feeling dropped into the pit of her stomach. It wasn't unusual for Charles to hardly be at work, but to know they were celebrating something she didn't know about, worried her.

Once again a surge of panic erupted that Charles may have somehow sold the business without her even knowing, before she once again reassured herself safe in the knowledge no one had been in touch to get any financials or to do any kind of due diligence. She also took comfort in knowing without a doubt, Charles didn't know how to retrieve the information from the computer. So what on earth was going on? Silently she prayed they were only going to celebrate the purchase of a new car or some other unnecessary or frivolous thing. However, until she found out the answer, her stress levels once again skyrocketed.

All day while Jacqui was at the office on edge and wound tighter than a spring, Charles couldn't help but rub his hands with glee, the dollar signs gleaming like neon in his eyes. Very soon, he was about to be free and very, very rich.

At the offices of Duncan Dell & Partners where the deal was to be signed, Charles could barely contain his excitement. Even his own lawyers were in awe of being in such prestigious offices when theirs were nowhere near as fancy. When they received the paperwork, they could see nothing wrong with it, but in truth, no one from their office had in experience of dealing with such a big transaction so even if everything wasn't in order, they would never have noticed.

"Gentlemen, sorry to keep you waiting," Brad Duncan said, greeting his visitors and leading them to a conference room.

Charles' lawyers were stunned to be greeted by one of the partners of the prestigious firm. They expected just another lawyer handling the deal. A frisson of excitement shot through them that this was the big time. It didn't matter there was no negotiating involved, this was still a momentous occasion for them.

Inside the conference room, Trevor was already there, and greetings were exchanged.

"So we are all in agreement then for this sale?" Brad said, as nodding assent went around the room. "Great, let's get to the signing."

Charles went first and had to still his shaky hand, while trying hard to hide the giddiness and elation he felt as it was nearly over.

There was a knock at the door and a young Asian man dressed in a sharp black suit walked in. Charles felt a brief moment of anxiety that this man was about to somehow call a halt to the sale.

Boston could see the confusion on Charles and his team's faces, and only acknowledged them with a nod before signing where Brad pointed, then Boston made a call to the bank.

"Gentlemen, let me introduce the new owner of Aurora. He's managed to make time in his busy schedule to sign and ensure the transfer of the money," Brad said.

Charles' head spun in confusion. He thought Trevor Sacks was the buyer. Did it matter? No, he didn't care who bought Aurora, just that the deal had gone through.

"The money has been authorised and should be in your bank account within a few days," Boston said. "Gentlemen it was great doing business with you. Trevor, I'll talk to you later. Brad, good job. I'll let Jason know."

Trevor just sat there and grinned, knowing he'd be seeing Boston very shortly. Brad smiled knowing one of his biggest clients was happy.

Charles' lawyers were still speechless and in awe of the man who had entered the room, signed, then authorised payment of such a huge amount of money and then departed. It was a story they'd be repeating for the rest of their lives.

"Charles, congratulations. You're now a very wealthy man and good luck for your future endeavours," Trevor said, shaking hands.

"Thank you and good luck to you with Aurora," Charles said.

Finally the deal was done and Charles could breathe again.

He was free.

Now it was time to celebrate.

Trevor was meeting Boston at a nearby restaurant and knew his brother, Phoenix would be joining them for lunch. He hadn't met Phoenix yet and once again briefly wondered if perhaps he was getting himself in over his head if Phoenix wasn't as quick on the uptake as he had been led to believe. The only reason he was now a doubting Thomas was because of the possible Charles and Jacqui Richmond deception. What if Phoenix was like Charles? His instinct told him if Boston was his brother, then Phoenix would be smart, but it wasn't always the case. What if Phoenix and he didn't get along? That would make this scenario a nightmare.

As the two men sat and relived their successful deal, Trevor decided it was time to bring up Phoenix.

"So before I meet your brother, what can you tell me about him? I'd just like a little background information to know how fast he'll cotton on since Lucas said he's never run a company before," he said, trying to be diplomatic.

"I think you need to ask Tony that question," Boston chuckled. "He's been his mentor from the start."

Trevor sighed, wishing he'd thought to do that, but his head spun with the quickness of this deal, and therefore it completely skipped his mind.

"Will do," he said. "However, do I ask how this is all going to work now you own Aurora? Is Phoenix going to suddenly be my second in command or a co-CEO?"

Lucas answered all these questions before Trevor agreed to the job but still, he wanted to make sure the arrangement hadn't changed before he started. He didn't want any surprises.

"As far as I'm concerned, and I know Jason and Lucas think the same, we don't want Phoenix thrown into the deep end. Not because he wouldn't succeed, but he needs the time and experience to grow into the role which was why Lucas thought of you," Boston said. "Personally, I think Phoenix should stay where he is or maybe move into the executive offices, but still keep a low profile."

Boston's chuckle made Trevor think he was quite enjoying the thought of having his brother do the paper shuffling.

"Perhaps you can go over things at night or have meetings? I'm not sure, but it's something you and Nix need to work out. He knows where we all stand on this and will back you if he thinks he can just jump in and run. He's not ready yet," Boston said.

Trevor sat there thoughtful, appreciating Boston's honesty. He had to admit he liked the way they did business. Even when they could have totally screwed Charles over, they hadn't. In fact, he wasn't even sure Charles realised they were also generously giving him all the profits made from this financial year.

"Here's Nix and Tony now," Boston said, as the two men stood to greet the newcomers.

Phoenix was totally overwhelmed to meet Trevor and relieved Tony and Trevor knew each other so the conversation never became stilted.

Trevor retold the tale of the deal for Tony's benefit with Boston adding they signed the papers this morning.

The lunch gave both Trevor and Phoenix a chance to not only get acquainted as everyone chatted, but had both men feeling more at ease with each other.

However, the lunch only managed to distract Phoenix for a short time from worrying about Jacqui. How would she react when Charles told her he sold? He knew she wouldn't take it well, but would she be able to handle all the emotions that came with it.

Boston said the money would soon be in Charles' bank account. Maybe he should check on her tomorrow night, but then he changed his mind. Phoenix didn't want to accidentally tell Jacqui if Charles hadn't done it. Her brother should be the one to break the news, not him.

Feeling like he was stuck in a state of limbo, he decided to wait until he could speak to Boston alone and get his thoughts on the matter.

"Do you think I should go and see her, make sure she's okay?" he said, concerned.

"Nix, we don't know when or even *if* Charles is even going to tell her. The man Trevor dealt with isn't exactly Mr Honest. He was skulking around with the deal, so do you really think he's going to tell his sister even a minute before he has too?" Boston said. "He sounds like a guy who would just leave work one day and never return, thus leaving everyone left to wonder where he went or what happened to him."

Well, when Boston put it that way, Phoenix thought, but still…

"I know you just want an excuse to see her, but if you end up accidentally telling her before her brother, well I just think it'll make things worse. Let him tell her, if he has the guts and then she can rage at him," Boston said.

"But she'll be crushed and need support," he said, knowing he was grasping at any straw to justify seeing Jacqui, but couldn't help it. She truly would be devastated by the news.

"Then either let her come to you or if you do happen to hear anything official, *then* you can go to her. Until then, stay out of it," Boston admonished. Seeing Phoenix was about to argue, he held up his hand. "I know you feel helpless, but this is *their* family and let's face it, the dynamics are not what we're used to. Just because we don't like what Charles did, it's not our problem. We can be there for her *when or if* she needs us."

"I hate it when you're right," he grumbled.

"I know," Boston grinned.

"Just like you sat back and waited for Lys to just come around," he said, knowing full well, Boston had only done that because he had been forced to.

"Exactly," Boston chuckled. "However, circumstances were different. Lys also had a meddling uncle and father to contend with, while I had you lot," Boston grinned.

"Love sucks, doesn't it?" he said, miserable.

"Only until you get the girl and then it's all rainbows and sunshine," Boston smiled.

The happiness on Boston's face made him laugh.

"Can't wait to see how you deal with a meddling uncle and father when the baby comes," he teased.

"Don't remind me." Boston heaved a sigh. "I think I'll just enjoy every minute until she announces it to them, then the smothering will begin, which won't bother me until she gets fed up with it and then it's all on me to have to deal with it."

"Maybe you should run away to New Zealand to have the baby. It's far, far away from them," he said.

"Good idea, only I don't think we can do that to her dad. Although a little holiday break there would delay any announcement, since we really should tell mum and dad and the brats in person," Boston laughed.

Chapter Sixteen

Charles waltzed into the office with a bright smile on his face and a spring in his step knowing today was possibly the last day he ever had to work in this wretched company. He was thankful Jacqui hadn't arrived yet, as he still wasn't sure how to break the news to her the company was sold.

After celebrating with Cynthia, Charles decided it needed to be discreetly handled because he knew Jacqui would yell the whole place down when she learned the news. He also had to break it to his father and therefore decided a family dinner, probably the last they would have for a long time, would be nice.

Cynthia of course cried off saying she had too much to organise if they wanted to leave by next Saturday.

Charles couldn't help but be relieved by his wife's absence knowing Cynthia wouldn't be of any help in this situation. She was more likely to inflame rather than contain his family's reaction. And because he was such a chicken, he waited until it was almost home time before talking to Jacqui about it.

All day Jacqui had been giving him questioning looks and repeatedly asked what he had been celebrating. He continually fobbed her off, but seeing his bank account with more zeros in it than he'd ever seen in his life, he was thankful Jacqui was away from her desk and didn't hear his shout of excitement.

"Jacs, I was going to have dinner with dad tonight, get his favourite takeaway. Want to come?" he said.

She eyed him suspiciously and wondered what he was up to. At least if they were in private, she could give him a piece of her mind and remind him about giving his word to wait and think about selling.

"Sounds great. Is Cynthia coming?" she said, trying to sound cheerful.

"No, she's busy. Can you order and pick it up?" he said.

"Sure," she said.

Typical Charles, she fumed. He has the idea for a family dinner, but then gets her to do all the running around for it. She was only thankful Cynthia wasn't coming as she always moaned about everything.

"I'm off to get dinner so I'll see you at dad's," she said poking her head into his office wondering why he was still here. Charles never stayed after five. Was he up to something?

"I'll see you there," he said, trying hard not to blurt out the truth while hiding his excitement that once he walked out the door tonight, he was never returning.

Reluctantly Jacqui left the office still wondering what Charles was up to. She could have asked, but was too scared to know the answer. Feeling uneasy and unsettled, she decided it would be better to confront him at their father's, where she wasn't going to let him get away until he answered *all* her questions.

Both Charles and Jacqui were on edge and anxious for their own reasons throughout the entire meal and by the time they finished, their anxieties ramped up. The tension they both held had them ready to snap.

"Dad, Jacs, I have some big exciting news. I sold the company," Charles beamed.

"You what!" she said, shocked.

Gene also looked stunned and speechless.

"But you said you'd wait a year," she said, furious.

"Well, what can I say, when the opportunity arose, I took it," he said, trying to stay staunch, but the feelings of guilt began creeping in.

Jacqui was so furious that she was determined for once to make her father see Charles wasn't the golden boy he thought he was.

"He sold the business! The one you started from nothing," she said, unable to contain her fury. "Your legacy. Gone!"

Assuming their father would be just as outraged as she was, she was dumbfounded when all he did was nod.

"Well, I'm sure he not only got a good price for it and I'll tell you what, once I get the money you can have a shopping spree or a new car. How's that?" Gene said.

Jacqui not only wanted to beat Charles to a pulp, but also slap her father very hard, such was the frustration and anger she felt right now at his calm acceptance the company he had founded and built up was now gone.

"That's another thing, dad. Cynthia and I have decided we want to live in Europe so I'll give you a few mill and Jacs can have her shopping spree, but that's all," Charles said. "I know you understand how expensive living there will be and we'll need every penny we can to be able to make the right contacts."

Jacqui's head spun at not only her brother's greed, but the fact he was going to waste it all on trying to live it up in Europe like the super wealthy just enraged her even more. This had to be all Cynthia's idea. She was the money hungry one of the two who wanted to live like money grew on trees while pretending she had blue-blood in her veins.

What was going to happen once the money ran out, which judging from Cynthia's taste would be quickly? She could only assume Charles would be dumped and divorced faster than he could add two and two and he wouldn't even see it coming, he was that much of an idiot.

Now Gene was not only flabbergasted, but his eyes widened and anger crossed his face at his son's declaration.

"That's my money!" he roared.

"Actually, it's not. You *gave* the company to me. You're lucky I'm willing to be generous since I actually don't have to give you a thing," Charles said, glad Cynthia wasn't here because she would have cut his family off without a single penny, but he couldn't be that callous and a little bit of guilt was also the reason he made the offer.

"Which you were supposed to run. Not sell!" Gene said, furious at his son's betrayal.

Jacqui was finally happy her father could now see his mistake, that Charles wasn't a loyal son.

"It's done." Charles shrugged. "Not much you can do about it now. Surely you must have realised I hated the business. Was no good at it?"

"Of course you were good at it." Gene said. "I wouldn't have turned it over to you if you hadn't been."

The laugh Charles gave made Jacqui dread what her brother was about to say.

"All these years I thought you would have realised the only reason I wanted Jacs as my secretary was because she did *all* the work. I couldn't do *any* of it. She's ten times smarter than me," he said.

Now the truth was finally out in the open, she waited with bated breath to see what her father would say. Would he finally give her, her due?

"Well that at least was smart, keeping it in the family. The business is sold so off you go and enjoy Europe," Gene said.

No one knew who was more astonished. Jacqui, because finally their father had heard the truth and still acted like it was Charles' right to lie and pretend he was better than he was, thus making the good choice to use his own sister. Or because even after announcing the truth, their father didn't care and still let Charles take all the credit and money, while she still didn't even get a second thought.

For the first time in her life Jacqui actually saw Charles redden in embarrassment for her. He couldn't hide his pitying look at their father's dismissal of Jacqui's participation and saw the sadness in her eyes that nothing she had done in all these years mattered and he felt guilty.

"Who did you sell it to and for how much? When do they take over?" she said, demanding answers.

"It's none of your business how much I got, but they take over from tomorrow," Charles said.

"Tomorrow?" she said, confused. "Normally it takes months to do the deal. No one's come to me to ask for financials or any due diligence information."

"They didn't need it. As soon as the money was in my account, it's their company," he said.

"So who are we expecting to come and take over your job? How would I know they're the actual owner?" She was still in a daze over Charles' answers, trying to comprehend his stupidity.

"Trevor Sacks," he said.

"Trevor Sacks?" Gene perked up at the name. "Well, at least that's good news. Trevor is a legend in business circles and he wanted my company. That's fantastic." His chest puffed up at the thought.

"Actually he was only negotiating on behalf of someone. I hadn't realised until we signed the deal, he wasn't going to be the actual owner," Charles blushed.

"So who's the new owner?" Gene said.

"Don't know," he shrugged. "This Asian guy came waltzing in, signed the papers, made a call to his bank and then waltzed out. It was pretty impressive."

Asian guy? Her mind whirled. Could it have been Phoenix? He said his family were about to make an offer. Had he somehow shafted her brother and pulled the wool over his eyes? And how did Trevor Sacks enter the equation? She knew his name well enough to know how respected he was in the business world. There seemed to be more questions than answers sprinting through her head, but she needed to put those to one side for now and concentrate on getting more answers from Charles.

"I can't believe how selfish you are! All these years I've done everything for you and this is how you repay dad and I, by not only selling up, but then leaving the country and us with nothing?" she shouted.

"Get off your high horse, Jacs," he said. "You could have left at any time, but you didn't. You didn't have to keep being my lackey. In fact, if you had stopped years ago then perhaps dad would have seen the truth and not given me the company and then none of this would have happened."

"How dare you? I did this for you because family helps each other," she said.

"No, you wanted to be the martyr. You've been so hung up on trying to get dad's approval, that's why you hung in there. It wasn't for me," he sneered, hitting her with a few home truths. "If you had left and been a success on your own while I floundered, then dad would have had no choice but to acknowledge you were smarter, even if he still didn't let you run the company. But instead, you hid behind me."

"And now you've hung me out to dry too. Thanks to you

I've probably lost my job, did you ever think about that? I've bills to pay too, you know," she said.

Pink slashed across Charles' cheeks, but then he laughed making her even angrier.

"Come off it, Jacs. You're not hurting for money. Why do you think I kept giving in to all your ridiculous demands for a pay rise? You're earning far more than me. I did it because I knew you deserved it, so don't go around acting like some kind of wounded heroine. You're not. You're paid more than all the assistants in the entire world and a lot of CEOs," he said.

The wind was taken out of her sails because what Charles said was the truth. She would demand exorbitant pay rises from him and he would always give in. At the time, she felt it was not only her due, but was a way to punish her brother and father.

Why had she never left the company? She thought about it in the early days, and if she had as Charles said, then perhaps her father would have had to acknowledge she had the smart genes and Charles didn't.

Charles hit his target with precision. She had done all this in the hopes she would finally get their father's approval and acknowledgement, only now to realise she was never going to get it.

Had she been wasting her life on a pipe dream? Or had she just become so comfortable hiding behind Charles' name and therefore been too scared to go out in the real world and do it as herself?

"So you'll be in tomorrow to introduce everyone —"

"No. I've cleared out my office. It's now up to you. I'm not going back," he said. "Next Saturday, Cynthia and I are off to Europe for good. We'll send you our details when we've set ourselves up."

"B-but what am I supposed to tell our employees? Clients?" she said, stunned.

"Don't know and don't care. I'm finally free of that millstone around my neck and want nothing more to do with it. And, don't worry Jacqui. I'll sort you. It's the least I can do," he said, before leaving the house.

Gene watched his son leave and then ignored her to go and watch TV. That's what hurt the most. He still didn't give her any credit for all she did for him or Charles, or the business.

No acknowledgement at all and that was worse than being thought a useless female. Her own father considered her a nobody.

Jacqui went home still dazed and confused over what had happened at dinner. It all seemed surreal, like it was a very bad dream or better yet, a nightmare. Had Charles truly just sold the business without any kind of negotiations? Had he just walked out of the company, never to return, not even for his things? No, he said he'd already cleared out his desk. No wonder he stayed late tonight and wanted Jacqui to pick up the dinner. He hadn't wanted her to see him doing it because they would have had words there and then.

How could he want to leave the country and not look back? That was probably Cynthia's idea. But to not even give their father any real money from the sale? Even though it was callous to her, right now she was still hurting over her father's reaction to Charles' confession.

She needed to desperately to talk to someone and her first thought was Phoenix. However, she realised if he was the one who took Charles for a ride, then she was not only playing into his hands, she would also be putty in them.

Then she remembered what Eddie said about Phoenix. That he would drop everything for a friend and she was sure if she called him, he would be at least sympathetic and understanding of the situation, but nothing would change. He won. She lost.

What about Eddie? He said she should call if she ever needed a friend or to catch up? Would he take this as a sign she wanted to be more than friends?

Round and round her brain whirled until she thought she was going crazy. Then she grabbed her phone and made a call.

Well that should never have happened. Unbeknownst to the other they were both thinking the same thing and came up with the same answer. Not only had the sex been as spectacular as they both remembered, neither could regret it.

"You know I hadn't meant to seduce you. I was just wanting someone —"

He silenced her with a kiss.

"I know. But I don't regret it, do you?" he said.

"No." She shook her head knowing she'd just lied to them both. She had wanted to seduce Phoenix otherwise she would never have invited him over. Should she confess?

"Well, perhaps I may have —" she said.

Once again he silenced her with an even more thorough kiss than the last one.

"I know. I would have still come just to be your shoulder and if you were to offer more…" he said.

She smiled they were both on the same wavelength. It seemed to make what she needed to say so much easier.

"You know I was thinking since Aurora's been sold and I'm assuming it was your family who bought it. What do you say you and I go halves and we start up our own company?" she said.

"Our own company?" he said, confused.

"Yes. We both know finance so why don't we start from scratch as partners. I mean, I know you've definitely got the nous to make it a success —"

"You know?" A stunned look appeared on his face.

"Yes," she blushed. "I may have peeked at your personnel file and snooped about the investment department, which has gone from strength to strength since you came on board."

"What else do you know?" he said, feeling like the ground was now quickly turning into quicksand.

"That Boston is also really rich," she said.

"You snooped on my brother? When?" he said.

"After our last argument." She reddened again. "I couldn't work out how your family could afford such an expensive company, so I googled him and found out he's done really well for himself and is really wealthy. No wonder the banks would loan him that kind of money."

The more Jacqui spoke, the more of a nightmare this was becoming. Charles obviously hadn't told her just how much he sold it for. He scrubbed his face with his hand and then raked it through his hair trying to keep calm.

"So what do you think? We can start a new company and become even bigger than Aurora. I'll run it and you can do all the wheeling and dealing," she smiled.

That's when a light shone on the truth. Jacqui just wanted to be able to run her own company. She may have accepted she was never going to do it with Aurora, especially now that it was sold. And since she knew he was not only a whiz with numbers but successful, she wanted him to give her back what she had just lost.

"I think you've misunderstood," he said, his throat closing up as the words became stuck. "I'm going to be running Aurora."

"What? Don't be ridiculous. I mean, I know your brother bought the company, but you know nothing about running a multi-million dollar company," she said.

"I know, that's why it's not happening overnight. It'll take some time, but eventually its mine. Why else do you think my family bought it?" he said.

Oh God, she was an idiot. She had totally forgotten what he'd previously told her. Here she had been thinking they could both build something together so when she finally became even more successful than Aurora, she could throw it in her father's face, but now Phoenix had betrayed her all over again.

"So you've used me once again," she said, choking on her bitterness.

"Jacs, it's not like that. Like I said, I would have come to just be your shoulder —"

"Liar!" she said, angry.

"Oh no you don't. You don't get to be the holier than thou one. Like I conned you. I didn't con you. Last time I was upfront about what was happening. You deserved to know the rug was being pulled out from under you. And tonight, you just admitted you wanted it just as much as me, so you don't get to pretend I was the one lying just to get you into bed. You're just as big a liar as me," he raged, trying to find his clothes. "And, don't think I don't realise you wanting to start a new company and make it even more successful than Aurora is just about you still trying to prove to your father you're the smarter child. To throw it in his face. You said we'd be partners and yet, you've already put yourself in the driver's seat. Captain of the ship. All you want is to run your own company, and if you didn't need me, I wouldn't even rate a thought."

"Get out!"

"Gladly," he said. "You know, at some stage you're going to have to get rid of that massive boulder on your shoulder. Charles isn't there to blame anymore, nor is your father. Who are you going to blame for your life now?"

His hand was on the doorknob as he turned and looked at her.

"Oh, and one more thing before you blame my family for swindling Charles, because I'm sure that's what you'll do in your need to have someone to blame. All he wanted was cash in the hand. He didn't care about the company, the employees or anything. Just the money. So while you're cursing me and my family for their good fortune at seeing an opportunity and taking it. You should be glad it was us and not someone stripping it down or firing everyone," he said.

Quietly he left and she burst into tears, hating him.

Chapter Seventeen

Few things in the business world shocked Trevor these days as he had been and seen most of it after being in business all his life. Needless to say that he was finally shocked speechless was an understatement.

Turning up at Aurora at ten to see Charles and discuss how he wanted to handle the handover, he was informed by Jacqui Richmond that Charles had not only left the building never to return, but also not made any announcement or plans to announce the new ownership.

"I'm so sorry all this has been handled so chaotically," she said, embarrassed.

Trevor raked a hand through his hair, wondering how they were both so calm and yet, mindful of what was about to happen.

"It's not your fault, any more than it's mine. I guess you'd better bring me up to speed so we can sort out an announcement. I'll also need to see all management…" He looked at his watch. "Let's say at four, that should give us some time to sort some kind of plan. It would have been nicer to have organised this earlier, but this will have to do," he said, not wanting to say that they were both blindsided by Charles' actions.

"Great. Let me just grab some coffees and make sure we're not disturbed. I'll be right back," she said.

"Oh, and Jacqui?" he said.

"Yes?" she said, turning to look at him.

"Thank you for understanding, I know how uncomfortable this must be for you and you may not want to be here right now, but I do appreciate it," he said.

She nodded before leaving his office, glad he wouldn't see her cry.

Once Jacqui left, Trevor lent back in his chair deep in thought trying to make some sort of game plan. Clearly Charles had been very serious when he said once he received his money, the company was theirs.

Thankfully, once they were both over their mutual embarrassment at the turn of events and knowing Jacqui was willing to work with him, they both rolled up their sleeves and got down to business.

One week later, Trevor called Jacqui into his office.

"You wanted to see me?" she said, sitting in the chair in front of his desk.

"Yes. I have a couple of serious questions for you and it is your right not to answer, although it would help provide some clarity," he said.

She squirmed in her seat and knew what he was about to ask and didn't know whether she wanted to admit the truth or not. Surely Phoenix would have told him, or was this just his way of playing dumb to see how honest she would be? Now she found herself tangled up in knots.

All this time having never seen Phoenix at work or even in the building, lately he seemed to be almost haunting her everywhere. Jacqui could almost swear she smelt his cologne when she arrived in the mornings, and knew it wasn't Trevor's scent. Then there were the times she saw him wanting to catch the elevator and she was already in it. He would glance in, see her and then pretend to take a call or miss it completely. Those times hurt more than she could say. He seemed to have the same solemn look on his face too.

She shook her head to focus back on Trevor.

"What did you want to ask?" she said, nervous.

"I've been here for a week now and thanks to your excellent help and assistance even though I know this must be extremely tough, I want you to know I appreciate it," he said.

She exhaled a breath of relief and relaxed.

"However, I've noted your renumeration is a lot more than any executive assistant and CEO joined together and if Charles wasn't your brother, I may have thought along some devious or even very inappropriate lines of thinking. So why are you paid so much more than Charles?" he said, knowing he probably knew, but wanted to see if she'd tell him the truth or not.

Did she tell him the truth or not? Surely if he did the deal with Charles then Trevor would know Charles wasn't smart or business savvy.

"Charles was more of a figurehead since it was my father who started this company and him being his son. I did all the day to day running of the operation," she said.

"I figured as much just by all your knowledge," he said, knowing she was only being diplomatic and clearly not wanting to badmouth Charles. "And just out of curiosity, if you had been the one to sell the company, how much would have you wanted for it?" he said.

"I'll be honest, I don't actually know how much Charles sold it for. I'm guessing it'll come out in the next quarter or end of year reports."

The look of astonishment on Trevor's face showed he had no idea Charles wouldn't have shared the information with his family.

"This is a very solid company, which is also making some great in-roads here so at a conservative estimate, I wouldn't have sold for less than thirty to forty million," she said.

He whistled at her figure.

"You think someone would have paid that much for possible growth and potential?" he said.

"Yes, especially if someone approached me out of the blue. All our figures show we're growing quite rapidly, especially our investment division," she said, pleased she sounded normal and calm. "I honestly don't think it would take too long for it to reach or even surpass that kind of value at our current trajectory. Besides, whoever bought it, I'm sure they would have their own contacts which could boost the company's value even faster, that's if they didn't just swallow up our company and merge it into theirs. Therefore I would have either held off on selling for another few years if possible, to get my numbers a lot better or I would have possibly put it out for tender. Get a bidding war, hopefully push the price up over fifty million to hopefully say seventy. That's if the stars were all aligned, of course," she said.

"Wow, that's pretty ballsy. I'm not sure even I would pay that much on the possible future. But you're right on one hand, this company does have a lot of potential which would have attracted a lot of buyers, which as you say, if you got a bidding war, could be quite the financial windfall," he said.

Now he knew for sure Jacqui had all the brains in the family. Had she been in charge of the sales negotiations, it would have been a long drawn out expensive fight, but worth it in the end. Once again, he thought about how lucky the men who bought Aurora were.

She felt almost vindicated by Trevor's acceptance of her answer and that he hadn't laughed her out of his office and thought her crazy.

"That leads me to my next question? Just why have you been your brother's executive assistant all this time? You could have headed up any of the departments in the company. You clearly have the brains for it or at least been on the executive team," he said. "You could have even struck out on your own and made a name for yourself whether at another company or started your own business? So just what is it that you want from your life and career, Jacqui Richmond because even I can sense from knowing you this short time that you don't really want to be here."

His words took her by surprise.

"And when I mean here, I mean, this position. Yes, you're super efficient and yet, you don't actually seem like you enjoy the work and even with the autonomy of being the *de facto* CEO, you still don't look happy," he said.

She could feel the tears welling up and was trying hard to blink them back. What was happening to her? First Phoenix and now Trevor. Both seemed to understand something about her she didn't even know about herself.

She didn't expect to become so emotional, but Trevor was clearly some kind of magician who could see into her soul and knew the truth. She didn't like running the company. It was so stressful, not that Charles knew or cared. However, she had been so focused on that gold ring for so long, now that it had been taken away, she felt all the walls and structures she put in place to keep her motivated, crumbling faster than an avalanche.

Trevor felt awful seeing Jacqui tear up and walked around his desk to hand her his handkerchief.

"Thank you," she said, wiping her eyes. "I have no idea why I'm crying."

"Perhaps it's because what you've known and been doing for so long has reached that fork in the road. Believe me, I know what it's like to reach for something and not quite get there. Sometimes you think you're a failure, or it's not at all what you thought it would be. Other times you think you're lucky and had a near miss, but being on that road for so long, it's hard to deviate. So you just keep going along," he said.

She nodded at his wisdom. He was right.

"You're smart, Jacqui. Smarter than a lot of people I know and if you want to work in any of the departments just say the word. This company would be lucky to retain you. I don't want you to feel like it's a demotion or you're being pushed out," he said. "Well, you kind of are being pushed out, but only because a proper CEO would actually be taking a lot of your job back and they'd get an assistant who is just that, an assistant. And a lot more lowly paid one than you," he chuckled, as she smiled.

"Can't I just stay a very highly overpaid assistant then?" she teased.

"No, because then people truly would be thinking the wrong things," he smiled. "Rumours like that, a company doesn't need."

A week later as Trevor stepped off the elevator, he couldn't miss hearing Jacqui yelling along with her slamming and banging.

"Are you freakin' kidding me?" she said.

Unsure what set her off, as soon as she saw him, she was marching his way furiously waving paper.

"Is this true?" she said, still waving the paper, following him into his office.

"Is what true?" He was still unsure what had gotten her so riled up. Lately she had been miserable and flat and he hoped it wasn't because of their talk.

Torn between yelling at just what had her so infuriated and not yelling at her boss or wanting anyone else to hear, she gritted her teeth and waited until they were in his office.

"This." She jabbed at the paper she put in front of him. "Did Charles really sell the company for *this*?"

Now everything made sense. Jacqui had just seen the figure and realised how much Charles undervalued Aurora when he sold it.

"Yes," he said.

She instantly deflated and sagged into the chair, propping her head up, which now felt like a bowling ball.

"Please tell me the truth," she said, looking at him with misty eyes. "Did you play hardball and negotiate him down?"

He could hear the pain in her voice and his heart went out to her.

"I'm sorry, Jacqui. While I really want to lie, it would only be for your benefit. There was no hard ball involved, although I did offer a little fib and he obviously bought it," he said.

"No, I'm sorry my brother's an imbecile. I mean, it was your good fortune and knowing Charles, he would have really thought he was getting more than he actually thought the company was worth, that he was making a great deal," she said, tears falling.

"Probably," he nodded. After dealing with Charles and Jacqui and understanding their relationship, when Trevor thought back to their original lunch, now he understood why Charles acted the way he had.

"So what Phoenix said was true. Charles truly didn't try to negotiate any terms, didn't think about the employees or what his brother wanted to do with Aurora. He just wanted the money and ran," she said.

"You've talked to Phoenix?" he said, shocked.

The surprised look on Trevor's face made her want to laugh.

"Yes. He told me his brother bought the company for him to learn to run," she said.

"It sounds like you two are a lot closer than anyone would have guessed." Even him, Trevor thought. To be honest, he didn't even think they knew each other at all.

"Not any more. He tried to do the right thing by warning me, and I just spat the dummy. Then he tried to tell me Charles truly hadn't cared about anything, but the money and I got mad at him for that as well. But now…" she sighed. "I guess I truly can't pretend any longer my brother isn't just plain stupid."

"I'm really sorry, Jacqui," he said.

"Don't be," she said, dismissively waving her hand. "If I'm being honest I've always known it, but was too busy silently lording it over him that I could run circles around him with my eyes closed to care whether he was happy in the job or not. No, that's not true, I knew he was unhappy, but I didn't care either because I was happy being a martyr. Now look where all this has gotten us."

Trevor sat there quietly wondering where all this self-reflection was coming from. He knew he hit a few home truths with Jacqui and it seemed Phoenix must have too, and his heart went out to her. She truly was at a crossroads in her life.

For the first time in what seemed like for ever, Jacqui was leaving the office feeling more light-hearted than usual. She was also meeting up with Eddie.

"I'm so glad you called. I thought you crossed me off your dating list," he smiled.

"You were a question mark," she teased. "And I'm glad I rang. I needed to hear a friendly voice and you were the perfect antidote."

"Ouch, I don't know whether that's a compliment or I'm now in the friend zone," he said.

"Tell you what, let's have dinner and then we'll see if you're able to move out of the friend zone," she said.

The smile which lit up his face made Jacqui realise she had made the right decision to call Eddie. He was the perfect tonic to help her overcome this bump in her life.

"Let's see if I can make a start now," he said, and bent to kiss her.

She wrapped her arms around his neck not caring that they were standing on the street.

Reluctantly, he pulled back as they both smiled.

"I think that's a great start. However, a lot more persuasion will be required," she said.

"Still want to go to dinner or just skip to the privacy and persuading?" he said, his eyes filled with desire.

She was so tempted to jump straight to dessert, but wasn't quite in the right frame of mind yet.

"I think a little dinner and ambience would help lower my inhibitions," she said.

"Then let's get going," he said

Unbeknownst to Jacqui, Phoenix just happened to be across the street picking up some takeout to take back to the office. It's what he had done since Trevor started. Together they would eat and work after hours to try and get Phoenix up to speed on all things managerial. Of course, nothing could prepare him for the actual hands-on day to day running, but at least by the time he was ready, clients and employees would have confidence in his abilities. Tony joined them one night and offered to let Phoenix do his job on the sly so he could test out what he learned. They weren't too sure how it was going to work, but they'd find a way to make it happen.

Now the sight across the road struck him with a heavy blow to the stomach. Jacqui was kissing Eddie and smiling.

So Eddie had managed to catch up with her and by the looks of it, they had hit it off quite well, he thought miserably.

Back in his youth, he would have stormed over to the couple and confronted them, and it would have been more his jealousy, which would have made him punch Eddie, friend or not. Now that he was more mature, he managed to squash down his initial instinct to revert back to his youth to try and be happy for Eddie and Jacqui.

Brooding and trying to get his feelings under control he went back to work, but his mind just couldn't focus.

"Okay Nix, what's up with you tonight?" Trevor said. "Normally you have this laser focus and a million questions, but tonight you're just a big blob. Maybe we should take Friday's off, then you can go and let off some steam."

"No, it's okay, I just saw a friend and it threw me a bit,

that's all," he said.

Reading between the lines, Trevor could see *friend* was a euphemism for ex-girlfriend or perhaps someone he was keen on. Seeing how Phoenix really wasn't focused, he decided to use tonight to really get to know Boston's brother.

"So tell me about yourself?" he said.

"Huh?" Phoenix said.

"I said, 'tell me about yourself'. I know practically nothing about you except you truly are a whiz with numbers, have got a great head for investments, and a quick study. You're Boston's brother, related to Jason and Lucas and Tony's protégé. So tell me about yourself," Trevor said.

What did he have to lose, beside he could use the distraction, Phoenix thought.

After listening to Phoenix, Trevor could see he was a very talented young man with a very bright and promising future, yet he never mentioned girlfriends, not that he was judging.

"So what about your personal life? Do you have a significant other?" he said, wondering if he was pushing the envelope a little too far by being nosy.

"No," he said, miserable. "I thought I found a girl, but life got a little complicated and messy. Now she's moved on."

"I'm sorry," Trevor said, wondering if the complication had something to do with Jacqui Richmond. "So tell me about when you first moved over here and JJ. Tony mentioned something about crushing your opponent into dust," he said, trying to lighten the mood.

Phoenix laughed as he happily regaled Trevor with the story, forgetting about what he saw earlier.

Chapter Eighteen

"Hi Alf," she said, walking into the store.

"Jacs, my favourite customer, where have you been?" he said.

"Moping and hiding," she said, miserable.

"Why? From who? Your mother mentioned Charles sold the business and took off to Europe," he said.

"Yes, that's true," she sighed. "No, I waited just like you said Alf and thought I had found a great guy."

"So what happened?" he said, concerned and she was grateful he cared.

"Well, Eddie —"

"Eddie? My Eddie? Blind date Eddie, that Eddie?" he said, melodramatic.

"Yes, that Eddie," she laughed.

"Whoo hoo, go me," he smiled.

"As I was *saying*," she grinned. "We started dating."

The smile on Alf's face got even wider.

"But then he got this incredible job offer on the West Coast and couldn't turn it down and so now he's moved out there," she said. glum.

"His father hasn't said anything," Alf frowned. "I just spoke to Colin a few days ago."

"Apparently they're not happy with him because you know, Nina's just had the twins and they're a close family," she said.

"But that doesn't mean Eddie can't keep in touch or come back and see them. I mean these days with all the technology available…" he said.

"I know, but that's also why we broke up because it would be so hard to try and see each other. I don't want a boyfriend I only rarely get to see in person. I want someone here with me. You know, to cuddle, my comfy pair of slippers," she said.

She didn't say Eddie asked her to go with him and that she had not only been too chicken, but knew deep down Eddie wasn't the one for her. She was only trying to plaster over the cracks in her heart.

"I get that. It is harder in a romantic relationship to be apart. Honestly I wouldn't have thought Colin or Eileen would even notice Eddie wasn't there since they're both too busy smothering the twins," he chuckled.

"To be honest, I think that's also why he wanted to go. Perhaps not being there, they'd be happier to see him when he did make it back, if you know what I mean," she said.

"Sure do," he said. "So what can I get for you today?'

"Comfort food," she said.

"Dessert?" he said.

"Got myself a big slice of cheesecake waiting."

"Go with the eye filet then."

"I'm not celebrating" she said, confused.

"I know, but because it's so decadent, it'll cheer you up. Just make sure you don't overcook it," he grinned.

"It was *one* time, Alf. One time. Years ago. Let it go," she scowled, as they both remembered when she first started to cook for herself and she hadn't realised how to cook steak properly. It came out black all over and dry and chewy on the inside.

"I've given you two pieces, just in case," he winked.

She smiled, giving him a dramatic huff before stomping off to his chuckle.

What Jacqui had told Alf was the truth. When she started dating Eddie, she thought her life was finally back on track after all the upheaval, but as the relationship moved along, she sensed something was missing and didn't want to admit to it.

When Eddie told her he'd received a job offer on the West Coast, Jacqui couldn't help but be relieved. Now she could break up with him amicably until he asked her to come with him.

She tried to politely tell him it was impossible. Unfortunately he knew, thanks to her own big mouth, she was about to be out of a job soon and continued to try and persuade her go on an adventure with him.

Although she didn't know what she was going to do with

her life, she knew it wasn't with Eddie and so she broke it off with him, wishing him all the best, but it wasn't with her.

His sad face almost made her change her mind, but she stayed strong. Now she had heard from him and he seemed to be enjoying the change of scenery, she knew she had made the right decision. At first, he still lamented she wasn't there with him, but then the tone of his emails changed and she knew he was fine.

While she may have helped set Eddie free, she was beyond miserable and clearly not thinking straight. It was the only explanation as to how she was back to dating the wrong guys *again*.

Thanks to her mother and what Fleur considered a successful blind date with Mabel's help, this time it was Fleur's friend, Sonya Edmonds who swore her son would be just perfect for Jacqui.

Honestly if it hadn't been for her mother's continual nagging, Jacqui probably would have put her foot down and declined the blind date, but since she was still miserable about her life, she gave in.

Apart from Linda's blind date, the original one which set the whole blind date ball rolling and had been a complete disaster, the others were great. Even Alf's initial blind date with Eddie was only a bust from the point of view it was the wrong dinner companion. Thus Jacqui figured if she gave Sonya's blind date a go and it was terrible, then she could forever decline to be set up again without feeling guilty.

Admittedly Franklin Edmonds was a great dinner companion to start. When Jacqui thought of the start, she really meant the first few minutes from the greeting each other to the ordering. After that it all went downhill faster than an avalanche as she became very irritated by the man.

"Franklin Edmonds is relieved he's sitting across from such a sexy woman. Franklin Edmonds thought you'd be plain and fat," he said.

Jacqui was completely speechless and unsure how to respond not only to his disgusting backhanded compliment, but her date talking in the third person also came as a big surprise.

Franklin took Jacqui's silence as counting herself lucky she was on a date with someone as hot as him who complimented her.

"So what do you do? I don't know anything about you except our mothers are friends," she said, trying hard to ignore his quirk, which was fast becoming very irritating.

"Franklin Edmonds works at Heddon Industries as a manager. Since our mothers are friends, Franklin Edmonds agreed to this date. A favour to my mother and the fact you are sexy and hot makes it so much easier," he said.

"So you can't get your own dates?" she said, feeling a little hypocritical.

"Franklin Edmonds dates tons of women. My mother said you haven't managed to find a *real* man and needed to experience what it was like to date a great man and then you might aim higher," he said.

"*Excuse me?*" Her anger was ready to explode at his explanation and giant ego.

"You're Franklin Edmond's pity date," he shrugged.

"*Pity date?*" she said, still trying very hard to control her emotions, especially her temper. "I am *not* a pity date."

"Don't worry about it." He shrugged again. "Once Franklin Edmonds fucks you, you'll not only be crying from the ecstasy you've never experienced, but you'll know what it's like to date a ten and be treated like a princess. You'll be begging for Franklin Edmonds to sleep with you again. All the women do since Franklin Edmonds is not only the king in bed, but also has a gigantic c—"

"I don't think we'll be sleeping together," she said, not wanting to hear any more of his repulsive words. Her hand now gripping the table hard to stop herself from punching the arrogant egotistical jerk or slugging him with her handbag.

"That's because you've probably only had quickies. You need a man with stamina and that's built like a horse, just like Franklin Edmonds. I bet you've never truly orgasmed either. With Franklin Edmonds, you'll have multiple orgasms and wish every man after me was me," he said.

Unable to believe just how insulting and crude the man sitting opposite her was being, not to mention his over-inflated ego, she took a deep breath and tried to change the conversation topic.

"Do you always refer to yourself in the third person?" she said, unable to take it anymore and wanting to add, *and make yourself sound like a pompous, arrogant arsehole*, but she managed to hold her tongue, for now.

"Of course," he said. "All the great men of the world referred to themselves in the third person."

Huh? Her mind went into overdrive. She'd never heard that one.

"Really? Like who?" she said, curious to know his answer, if he even had one.

He looked stunned by her scepticism of his word.

"Look, pretty girls like you don't understand how the world works. Your minds are just too empty to comprehend what it's like to be great. But don't worry, Franklin Edmonds looks upon this moment as a teaching lesson. To answer your question, Napoleon," he said.

Her jaw clenched and she truly was half a second away from punching his lights out with his insulting, condescending attitude.

"Napoleon?" she said, with a quirk in her lips trying hard not to laugh. "I have never heard, read or even seen any documentary or movie where Napoleon refers to himself in the third person. Have you got anyone else?"

She knew she was provoking him, but he was a jerk and she was actually enjoying seeing him get riled up. Did the man not even see how idiotic he sounded? Obviously not.

"Of course," he said, displeased she was not only doubting him, but also being argumentative. "The great men like Michael Jordan, Steve Jobs, Abraham Lincoln and obviously the great, Muhammad Ali all refer to themselves in the third person."

Now she couldn't contain herself and burst into laughter because he was actually serious.

"Are we living on the same planet?" she said, incredulous. "I'm pretty sure Michael Jordan, Steve Jobs and definitely Abraham Lincoln *never* spoke of themselves in the third person. Muhammad Ali, I not terribly sure on so I guess I'll have to give you a pass on that one."

Jacqui could see Franklin's face get angrier with her arguing.

"Franklin Edmonds doesn't like your tone and the fact you are pettily arguing over this. Great people are always being cut down by the haters and Franklin Edmonds refuses to let you do the same to him," he said.

"I am not pettily arguing over this. And besides," she hissed, standing. "You're not great. You're just a pompous, arrogant idiot."

With that she stalked off leaving Franklin Edmonds sitting alone at the table.

What a jerk, she thought angrily to herself. Yet another blind date which ended up a disaster.

What she couldn't understand was, was this how people actually saw her? They thought these idiots were the kind of man she should end up with? Then she silently apologised to Eddie and Phoenix since they were the exceptions.

After this debacle, at least now she had a proper excuse to tell her mother, no more blind dates. From now on, she'd find her own dates. No, scratch that, there'd be *no* more dates of any kind.

Phoenix was having lunch with Sofia, Lucas' sister who was in town with her boyfriend and since Louis was running late from a meeting, she was happy to wax lyrical about him.

"I can't wait for you to meet Louis. He's a French god," she giggled.

"Okay, way too much information there. Is it even safe to have lunch in public if you're going to be smooching and throwing yourself at him all through it?" he teased.

"I knew you'd be jealous," she grinned. "If only you were a few years older, then I might possibly trade in Louis for you."

"No thanks," he shivered. "That would be like dating my sister."

"That is true. Did I tell you I saw Indi and Boston before I came rushing to your side?" she said.

Phoenix liked Sofia. Maybe it was because she was Lucas' younger sister and had a great sense of humour, or maybe it was because she was good friends with Indi ever since they spent months travelling around Europe together.

Now he understood why Sofia was so insistent upon catching up with him. His family sent her as their spy.

"Let me guess, they gave you some sob story about how lonely I was and you were to discreetly check up on me?" he said.

"Sì, but they said you'd see it coming a mile away so to just to attack the situation head on. So how are you? Any closer to getting this woman you pine for?" she said.

"I'm fine and the short answer is no. I saw her kissing someone else," he said, refusing to acknowledge it was not only a friend of his, but how much it hurt.

"Dio mio, you poor thing. No wonder you are sad," she said.

"It's fine, Sof. Oh look, there's a French god walking this way. Is this him? Is this Louis, your French god? I think I can hear angels singing," he teased.

"Sì, it is my French god. Perhaps he might have a French goddess for you?" Sofia laughed.

"I'm all for it, if she's a model," he chuckled.

"Men," she huffed. "No substance, just looks."

"Says the woman who keeps referring to Louis as a French god," he grinned.

They had a nice lunch and Louis was a great guy. Sofia also dropped a lot of hints that should Lucas ask Phoenix's opinion, Louis should be given a glowing review to her brother. Considering the couple had only been dating for a few months, Phoenix wasn't sure if it was love, but they seemed happy.

"Chérie, tomorrow I am swamped with meetings, will you be all right by yourself?" Louis said.

"Of course, I shall continue my shopping," Sofia smiled.

"Actually that would be perfect, Sof," Phoenix said. "I wanted to buy my brothers a thank you present and don't know what to get them. I mean, they have everything they could possibly want."

"How about an exotic dancer each?" she said.

"What?" Louis and Phoenix's faces were shocked by her answer and Sofia couldn't help but laugh.

"Well, you did say they had everything, so why not give them something different," she shrugged, like it was no big deal.

"Ah…" Phoenix was speechless.

"I'm just teasing," she said. "If you did that, *I'd* be shot and disowned."

"Phew, you did have me worried there," Phoenix said, relieved.

"Me too," Louis said, worried.

"Don't worry, I'm sure we can find them a boring, old tie or something like that," she grinned.

"How about a massive step up from a tie and a humongous step down from exotic dancer? There must be a perfectly happy medium somewhere and since you do like to shop, I know you'll come up with a great idea," Phoenix said, as Sofia beamed at him.

Chapter Nineteen

After getting Sofia's report, Montana and Indi had a video conference together and decided it was time to take matters into their own hands.

"What do you think we should do?" Indi said.

"Firstly we need to go to New York," Montana said.

"What's our reason and do we tell Nix we're in town?" she said.

Both sisters were thoughtful.

"I've got it," Indi said, excited.

"What?" Montana said.

"We need some sisterly bonding time with Lys. We'll just say that we want to take her on a weekend shopping break," she said.

"Ooh, that's a good one," Montana smiled. "I like it and Bossy won't mind either."

"But we have to make sure he doesn't come because knowing him, he'll invite himself," she scowled.

"True. The boys can have a boys' weekend together, with the kids, or not," Montana chuckled.

"I'm sure Jase will probably rope his family into helping and they'll be taken off his hands," she giggled.

"That's cheating," Montana admonished.

"Yes, but if your kids come over too, they'll also be invited. So really it's whatever gets us to New York and a weekend away is okay in my book," she said.

"Good point. Let's see if Lys is up for some Chan family meddling," Montana said.

Alyssa was more than excited to be a part of her first sibling relationship meddling, which amused Montana and Indi.

"After hearing your stories and living my own, I can't believe I finally get to be a part of one. This is so exciting. I thought only the boys got to do it," she said.

"Not this time. This time it's our turn to meddle and you're an integral part of the plan," Montana said.

"Well as soon as I mentioned it to Bos, he told Nix so I'm afraid Nix already knows we're coming," she said, apologetic.

"Lyssa!" Montana said.

"Lys!" Indi said.

"I'm sorry. How was I to know that Bos would be straight on the phone to Nix? But to be honest, I think it was more of a stern big brother warning to make sure nothing happens to us, rather than we're coming to meddle," she said, her explanation making her sisters-in-law scowl.

"Typical Bos," Montana huffed.

"Yeah, like we're five years old and don't know anything about the world," Indi said.

Alyssa had been around the Chan sisters long enough not to be frightened of their scowling and bossiness. Most of the times it actually made her laugh, especially when it was directed at their brothers.

"Well, since Nix knows we're coming, I guess we'll just openly interrogate him for more information. Sofia said he was still sad," Indi said.

"Right. We'll also need to work together to find out where Jacqui lives," Montana said.

"Why don't we just go to Aurora and hijack her from there," Alyssa giggled.

"That can be plan B," Indi laughed.

"I don't suppose he'd have her address in his phone and that way he won't even know we've got it?" Alyssa said.

"I'm not sure if that's crossing a line or not," Indi said, hesitant.

"True, but should he leave it open and lying around, I'm not above snooping," Montana grinned. "Besides, even if he catches us, this is for his own good. We need to know if she loves him back. After all, she is his *one*."

"Why don't we just tell him the truth? Surely it's in his best interests to have us meddle on his behalf and then he's got some sort of plausible deniability," Indi said.

"Listen to us. Snooping, plausible deniability, we sound like spies," Alyssa giggled.

"See how much fun we're going to have," Montana grinned, and the others couldn't help but agree.

Phoenix wasn't sure whether to be excited or dread having his sisters and Alyssa in town. They may have said they wanted a shopping weekend, but he had that funny feeling it was just a cover story. The real reason for them being here was to meddle and he wasn't sure how he felt about it.

He knew without a doubt Sofia would have told them he was still miserable. Would their meddling help him or completely turn Jacqui off? What about Eddie? He didn't want to purposely break up his friend's relationship with Jacqui, so perhaps he'd just see which way his sisters were heading before heading them off himself, or at least telling them they needed to leave Jacqui alone as she'd already found someone else.

"Nix!" Montana squealed, tightly hugging her brother.

"Nix!" Indi said, repeating the action. "We're so happy to see you. How are you?"

"I'm fine," he smiled, hugging Alyssa and was actually glad to see them now that they were standing in front of him.

"You still look miserable," Montana said, taking in his demeanour.

"Well, I'd be happier if it was Bos or the boys here, but since I've got you —"

"Nix! Don't make me box your ears already. We've only just got here," Montana huffed.

"Yes, and you don't have any back-up so I'd watch what

I say," Indi grinned.

"I'll tell Bos that you made me cry and you know he'll pummel you into the ground," Alyssa teased.

"Nice one, Lys," Indi giggled.

"Definitely one of us for sure," Montana laughed.

"And to think you were my favourite sister-in-law," he scowled.

"I'm your only sister-in-law and I haven't had this much fun in ages," Alyssa smiled.

"Clearly these two are a very bad influence on you. I'd better tell Bos," he said.

"He already knows," she giggled.

"I know when I'm beaten. Although I'm not sure if it's worse that you're doing it in my own home or not," he said.

"Well, we have a whole weekend of interrogating to do so you'd better buckle up," Montana said.

"Yes, there's no escape," Indi laughed.

"Oh, didn't I tell you? I have an urgent meeting somewhere else and have to leave you all, but it was good to see you," he teased.

They all tackled him and laughed.

He treated them all to dinner at a popular restaurant and realised how much he had missed them as he listened to them talk. It was different than being with Boston or his brothers-in-law. The women just seemed to be happy chatting about anything and of course making sure he was up to date on all the family gossip. It was a nice distraction from thinking about Jacqui and being miserable.

But it was back at Phoenix's that the conversation turned

more serious.

"So I guess you've heard that Vanna managed to guilt Lexi into staying at home with her instead of coming over to London?" Indi said, not entirely pleased by the news.

"What? Why? I thought Lexi was looking forward to coming?" he said, confused.

"Vans said she wanted them to do their OE together," she said, as everyone except Alyssa rolled their eyes.

"She does know she's being manipulated, right?" he said.

"Probably, but it also might suit her to stay. I don't know," she said.

"Maybe I should call her and see what's the deal?" he said.

"Don't do that, you might make her feel bad about it," she said, horrified. "I mean, I only know because I was excited to have my little sister stay with us and that's why she had to tell me her change of plan."

"Fine. I won't say a thing *for now*," he smiled.

"Anyway, so tell us all about Jacqui," Montana said, causing everyone whiplash at the topic change.

"There's not much to tell," he said.

"*Nix*." Indi and Montana scowled.

"It's true," he huffed. "She's moved on."

"Oh Nix, I'm so sorry," Montana said, sympathetic.

"Me too," Alyssa and Indi both said.

"Guess it wasn't meant to be," he shrugged, but still felt that ache in his heart.

"Don't say that. We all know she's your *one*. You'll end up together, we're sure of it," Indi said, confident.

"Yes, and we're happy to meddle and get the lay of the land. Find out if this guy she's supposedly dating is a serious thing or just a rebound fling," Montana said.

Phoenix could only wish it was a rebound thing, but after what he saw on the street that day, he wasn't so sure. If only it hadn't been Eddie and Nix didn't know what a great guy he was, then he would be more willing to try and steal Jacqui back.

"Consider this part of your story, the bump in the road," Indi said.

Somehow Phoenix couldn't see this as a bump, but more like a chasm in the road.

"We would love to meet her," Alyssa said, hesitant. "Let her get to know the family."

"Yes, great idea, Lys," Indi said.

"She'd love that," he sighed. "She's always wanted sisters or at least one sister. A hoard, I'm not so sure about." He tried offering a smile, but was flat.

"She doesn't have a sister?" Alyssa said, a little too excited. "That means she and I can be buddies."

"There you go, Lys, you'll have your own 'sister'," Montana laughed.

"I know. This is so exciting," she said, clapping her hands in excitement.

"If you give us her address, we can meet up with her to introduce ourselves," Montana said.

"Oh no, you guys aren't barging in on her unannounced. Just let her move on," he said, stern.

The woman exchanged a look.

"Fine," Montana sighed. "Do you at least have a picture of Jacqui? I'd love to know what she looks like."

Phoenix felt a shiver run through him. He could sense a trap, but didn't know where or what it was.

"Sure," he sighed. Opening his phone, he pulled up her smiling face. "Here."

"Ooh, she's pretty," she said, passing the phone to Indi and then moving to block her sister. "So tell me all about how it's going with Aurora? I heard you've changed it from Aurora Finance to Aurora International?"

"Yes, it gives the company more gravitas, don't you think?" he chuckled.

"I do. You'll be dominating all over the world in no time," she said.

As Phoenix gave his sister an update, unbeknownst to him, Indi sent a copy of Jacqui's contact details to Jason. She would have sent it to herself, but she didn't want Phoenix to realise what she had done.

Indi passed the phone to Alyssa after deleting her message to Jason.

"Hey, we should all come over to celebrate this deal together," she said, letting Montana know all was well.

"Great idea, Inds," Montana said.

"Yes, I'm sure Bos would love the idea too," Alyssa said.

"But we've already done it," he said.

Seeing the scowls on his sisters faces he knew he had just said the wrong thing.

"Exactly. *You've already done it*. And without us!" Montana huffed.

"Yes, Nix, that's so rude. We're your family too," Indi said, making her displeasure also known. "So how come we were left out?"

"It wasn't like that," he said, trying to placate two angry women.

"Oh, we *know* what it was like," Montana said.

"Fine, if it'll make you happy, we'll arrange something for everyone. Although it's really not necessary," he said.

"Of course it is," Montana said, happy they managed to wear Phoenix down. She wouldn't have put it past Phoenix to go all stubborn on them and refuse.

After all that subterfuge to get Jacqui's address, the women were all in agreement it was best to wait until their big get together to approach Jacqui. That way they could use the boys as a diversion and Phoenix wouldn't know what they were up.

Besides they needed time to plan how they were going to meet her and what to say. What if Jacqui wasn't interested in Phoenix anymore? Had really moved on or just wasn't willing to go back? They didn't want someone with Nix who they had to force to take him back or was with him for the wrong reasons. Even worse would be to get them back together only to find she had played them all along and was actually a gold-digger who was only after his money or wanted to try and get revenge, or get the company back.

Chapter Twenty

Once again Jacqui was miserable and it was all Phoenix's fault. She had been out running a few errands one lunch time when she spotted him with a woman who looked very beautiful and chic. Not to mention the way they were smiling and laughing together.

She told herself it wasn't jealousy she felt, but her heart ached nonetheless seeing him so happy. Part of her wished he could have at least looked just as miserable as she felt.

Ever since both Phoenix and Trevor hit it home to her that running the company wasn't something that she actually enjoyed, but rather something she did to prove herself to her father, her world had started to unravel.

Knowing she was soon to be unemployed and unsure of not only her future, but what her next step should be, Jacqui lay in bed miserable. She had spent so much time running Aurora and dreaming of the day she would get the accolades and title of CEO, that losing it was now giving her an identity crisis. Just who was Jacqui Richmond if she didn't work at or her family didn't own Aurora? This was all she had known her entire adult life.

That was why she needed a little time off and thankfully Trevor was happy for her to take a four day weekend.

She had planned to go away somewhere quiet. To be able to take a step back and reflect on all the upheaval which had happened in such a short amount of time. Even now, she only felt like the tornado was finally passing through her life, but what was left in its wake, well some things were devastated and other things just managed to only be a little damaged.

Maybe she should take some time out and travel the world, aimlessly wandering until she found another purpose or goal. As lovely as that sounded in movies or on TV, she just wasn't that kind of person. Holidays were one thing, but to just be nomadic wasn't in her DNA. It didn't mean she couldn't plan an extensive holiday.

Surely there were a lot of places in the world she really wanted to visit. Maybe she could start in New Zealand and then work her way back home. Sighing, she knew that was only because she wanted to see where Phoenix had grown up.

Trevor had negotiated a very generous severance package especially since she was happy to help train up her replacement and so she really had a few months still to ponder her next step.

The knock at her door had Jacqui wondering just who it could be since she wasn't expecting any visitors.

As she opened it, three beautiful Asian women stood there brightly smiling at her.

"Hi Jacqui? I know you don't know us, but we're wondering if you'd be interested in joining us for our spa day so we can get to know each other," one of the women said.

Jacqui blinked unable to comprehend three random strangers who knew her name were asking her to join them. It was creepy and a sliver of fear shot through her that she would be ending up in a body bag.

"Ah, I'm really sorry but —"

"Oh no, you've got it all wrong. Mon was supposed to introduce us, but in our excitement to finally meet you, she skipped that part," Indi said, glaring at her sister. "I'm Indi, Montana and Alyssa. We're Nix's sisters."

"His older sisters and sister-in-law," she said, relieved that perhaps she wasn't about to be murdered.

"You know about us? Nix has talked about us?" Montana said.

It wasn't surprising, yet the women were still delighted by the news.

"Probably nothing good," Indi grinned, earning her a nudge from her sister.

"Sort of. I've only managed to work out your names and Boston's, but not your younger sisters yet," she said.

"Oh, Lexi and Vanna are inconsequential," Montana said, dismissively waving her hand as the other women giggled. "Just don't tell them I said that, it'll start World War III."

"So will you come with us?" Alyssa said, with hope in her voice. "It'll be a great day getting pampered and chatting.

And we promise if you want to leave, we won't stop you. We just want to get to know Nix's future wife."

"Future wife?" She almost choked on the words. "I think there's been some kind of misunderstanding. I'm not his future wife. We don't even have a relationship."

"At the moment," Montana grinned.

"Yes. Believe me, once we've talked this all out, you'll see you're meant to be one of us," Indi said.

They were beginning to make it sound like some sort of cult.

"Does Nix know you're here?" she said, uncertain whether she meant in New York or on her doorstep.

"Yes and no. He knows we're in town and at a spa. We just didn't mention that we'd be dragging you along with us because you would have heard us arguing the entire way to your place. People probably would have called the police," Montana laughed.

"We wanted to meet you without Nix interfering, if you will," Indi said.

"Yes. How else are we supposed to meddle if he knows about it?" Montana giggled.

"What they said," Alyssa smiled. "This is my first time meddling and so far it's a cross between awkward and fun."

"But I'm dating someone," she lied.

"That's fine. Then just come with us as our new friend. You can tell us all about your new relationship and we promise not to try and change your mind about Nix," Montana said.

To Jacqui, this whole conversation seemed strange and

uncomfortable. She was trying to work out if they were completely overstepping boundaries or did actually have some hidden agenda. Phoenix had warned her his family were always up in each other's business whether they liked it or not. It wasn't that she hadn't believed him, but judging by today's surprise appearance it was not only true, but they also didn't look at all embarrassed about barging in on her at all. They actually seemed sincere.

To be honest, she did want to know what it would feel like to have sisters or pseudo-sisters and she could also pump them for information on Phoenix.

"Sure, I'll come. Why not? Besides, Nix did tell me the stories of how you all found your husbands and I have a lot of questions," she laughed.

After coercing Jacqui to join them and squealing in delight when she finally agreed, they excitedly headed to the spa where she then worked up enough courage to ask the question on her mind.

"Can I ask you all a question, it's a bit personal," she said, shy and hesitant.

"Of course," Montana said. "Our family motto is to be open with each other. It avoids a lot of fights and misunderstandings. If we don't want to answer, we'll tell you."

"Actually that's only one of our family's mottos. We have a lot that we pull out to suit any occasion so you'll hear that a lot, right Lys?" Indi said.

"Yes. Sometimes it's hard to keep up with and sometimes they even contradict other mottos," Alyssa giggled. "It's a Chan family thing that only they have. It's best to just go with it."

"Oh," Jacqui said, biting her lip. "I just wondered, I mean I know you have children, but did you want to stay home to look after them? What happens if you want to work?"

"Well, in my case, it helped that my best friends also had children so we hang out together a lot and I've never been a career-orientated woman," Montana said.

"And if I wanted to go back to work, then Jason wouldn't mind. We'd probably hire a nanny to help out, as the children are still quite young," Indi said.

"I don't have children yet," Alyssa said, rubbing her pregnant tummy. "But I know Boston doesn't mind what I do. To be honest, I'm dithering whether I want to continue to work or not. I'll probably just take maternity leave and then decide."

Their answers, as much as they were honest, didn't really help.

"To be honest Jacqui, everyone is different and every baby is different. If you had a child that needed more care and attention, it's a different decision to a child that's just super chill," Montana said. "Believe me, all my children are different and sometimes I wonder if they had been born in a different order, I may not have been so keen to be a mother so many times."

"And none of my pregnancies were so wonderful like in the movies," Indi said. "But when my baby arrives, they always seem so easy."

"I can't you tell you much, but I have the same anxieties as every other first-time mother about whether I'll be a good mother or not," Alyssa said.

"You will be," Montana and Indiana instantly said, making Alyssa smile.

"Yes, and you'll have us to talk to at anytime day or night," Montana said.

"And of course, most importantly, Nix would be there right beside you, supporting any decision you make," Indi said.

"From talking to some of the ladies at work, I know not everyone is cut out to be a stay-at-home mum. Some of the women find it so much easier to be at work or do part-time. So it's whatever works for you. Just because it works for someone else doesn't mean it works for you," Alyssa said.

"I guess what we're really trying to say, is that you won't know what you do or don't want or like until it actually happens. Unfortunately you can't test drive a baby and give it back if it doesn't suit, so you have to trust your partner to have your back," Montana said.

"Wow, I guess I hadn't really thought it was so complicated," Jacqui said.

"With the right guy, it's not complicated, but can still be a little messy," Indi laughed.

"Especially if you have parental hang-ups like I do," Alyssa said.

"What do you mean?" Jacqui said, curious.

"I had an absentee father most of my life. Then I had an uncle who turned up out of nowhere who tried to act like my father. But as a teenager, let's just say, it didn't go down too well," Alyssa said. "Even though I know I have Boston's support and love, it still scares me that I don't know how real parents are supposed to look or be, since I've never really seen it. However, being around Indi and Mon has helped me to see what a loving relationship and partnership should be, but I still worry."

Now all the women looked misty-eyed.

"I know what you mean. My father and mother are divorced and my father is a complete male chauvinist," she said.

Jacqui was soon spilling her life story explaining why Charles was left the business and not her and her duplicity as his executive assistant. She took heart in the fact that all the women were just as outraged as Phoenix had been on her behalf. Then she found herself telling them all about her disastrous boyfriends. In turn, they all shared their stories about meeting their husbands and Jacqui couldn't help but shake her head. It seemed Phoenix hadn't over embellished any of the retelling. If anything, he had undersold the stories.

Tears of laughter flowed and Jacqui finally felt like she had found a family, now she just had to hope it could have a happy ending.

"I'm so glad that I've got to meet you all and I do have a confession to make. I don't have a boyfriend," Jacqui said, knowing she should have been honest right from the start after seeing Nix's family keep their word about not pressuring her about him.

"We can all understand why you lied," Montana said.

"Honestly, I would have too, if three strangers turned up on my doorstep asking me to go to a spa," Indi giggled.

"Yes, we could have been total crazy women," Alyssa said.

"That's exactly what I thought," Jacqui laughed. "Your love stories are so romantic, I just wish that Nix and I could have that."

"But you can. Don't you see, if you guys get back together then you've also got a great love story to add to the family folklore. You're a perfect fit for our family," Montana said, as the others nodded.

"I'm still not so sure about that," she said, hesitant. "But I'm really glad you got me to come out today."

"Well, we're family so putting our noses in, welcomed or not, is the norm," Indi said.

"That's true. And, if you do marry Nix then I'll get to have my own 'sister' like these guys do," Alyssa smiled.

"Huh?" she said.

"Well, as you can see, the two eldest sisters have each other, as do the two youngest and the boys. However, should you marry Nix, then you and I get to be our own sisters especially since neither of us has one. But only if you wanted to," Alyssa quickly said, hoping she didn't sound too pushy.

Alyssa's words made Jacqui teary-eyed at the thought.

"I'd like that," she said, as Alyssa beamed.

"And I have to say, this is the first time us girls have really had a chance to meddle in our siblings' relationships. Usually the boys get all the fun," Montana said.

"Well, I did get to help get you and Lucas together," Indi grinned.

"Okay, Indi's the exception," Montana laughed. "I guess

the real question is, do you want to be with Nix? Do you love him?"

Jacqui wanted to say no, or that she didn't know, but deep down the truth was she did know the answer.

"Yes," she sighed.

Everyone's squeals of delight made her smile. This was exactly how she imagined having sisters or a close family to be. Seeing the way that Montana and Indiana included Alyssa was also heartwarming. Even from their few hours together, Jacqui knew that they'd be like that to her as well, that this wasn't an act for her benefit. They already were kind and supportive towards her and she didn't feel like it was insincere or they had an ulterior motive for it.

"Right, so now we plan on how to get you back together with Nix," Montana said.

"Oh, but does he even want to?" she said, hesitant.

"Of course he does. He's been miserable without you. Why? Did that big lug say something stupid to you?" Montana scowled.

"No, but I saw him have lunch with this glamorous woman," she said.

"That could just have been a business lunch," Montana said, waving a dismissive hand.

"They looked very happy and friendly," she said, still upset by it.

The looks exchanged by three of the women spoke volumes. Just because while they were sure Nix hadn't moved on with someone else, it didn't mean that he hadn't dated.

“I’m sorry, Jacqui. We don’t know what to say except that we’re sure Nix misses you, but that doesn’t mean he hasn’t dated. He said you had a new boyfriend?” Montana said, trying to get Jacqui to see they both dated.

“How?” she said, embarrassed that Phoenix knew about her and Eddie.

“Apparently he saw you together,” Montana said.

Jacqui burst into tears.

“I’m sorry,” she said.

“Don’t be,” Indi said, as they all hugged her. “We all get it.”

“Just like we all understand how guilty you feel knowing that he knows,” Alyssa said.

“Yes,” she nodded. “But it’s worse than that. It was with Eddie, Nix’s friend and the guy who was supposed to be my original blind date when I met Nix.”

Now Jacqui was upset she had inadvertently hurt Phoenix with his friend and even more glad she had broken up with Eddie.

“Believe me, Jacqui, I know how you feel. I slept with Boston and a fake Boston at the same time. The guilt is horrendous, but you have to let it go,” Alyssa said, sympathetic.

“You did?” she said.

Three sets of eyes and voices looked at Alyssa in astonishment and she reddened.

“Yes,” she said.

“Oh, this we didn’t know,” Montana giggled.

"Yes, now you have to spill?" Indi smiled. "Does Bos know?"

"Yes and no, but probably not all of it as such. So no telling," Alyssa said, her voice stern and the Chan sisters were delighted their sister-in-law truly was acting like one of the family.

"We promise," they said, as three sets of fingers crossed their hearts.

This only made Jacqui even happier knowing Alyssa understood her situation. Then an epiphany hit as she realised that neither of Phoenix's sisters judged Alyssa on her actions. They embraced her with sisterly love and Jacqui knew that this family was exactly what she had wanted all her life.

Chapter Twenty-one

After the most amazing spa day in which Phoenix's sisters and sister-in-law insisted Jacqui needed to not only boost her confidence, but also to get to know them better, Jacqui was now ready for her blind date with Phoenix. It was more of an ambush since he had no clue what was about to happen.

It not only boggled her mind as they debated the best way for Jacqui to reunite with Phoenix, but also warmed her heart they knew this would be a private moment between the two of them and didn't expect to be included. The tactfulness after all the meddling seemed like a contradiction. She was also impressed at how the women also managed to arrange tonight with their husbands without Phoenix realising.

Soon it would be the moment of truth. Did Phoenix truly love her or not? Despite his sisters' reassurances that he did, Jacqui was still full of nerves and anxiety churned her stomach into queasy knots.

“How are you doing?” Alyssa said.

“Great.” She gave a forced smile then promptly burst into tears making the three women rush to comfort her.

“What’s wrong?” Indi said.

“What if this doesn’t work? What if he really doesn’t love me or want me?” she sobbed.

“Then he’s an imbecile. A nincompoop. A bonehead,” Montana said.

That managed to get a smile out of Jacqui.

“But he’s your brother,” she said.

“Doesn’t mean we still can’t think he’s all those things,” Montana said. “Besides, we all know you’re the perfect woman for him and if you want, we’ll be quite happy to go and tell him so.”

“I know I’d enjoying smacking some sense into him,” Indi chuckled.

They turned to look at Alyssa.

“Oh, I’m new to the family so I don’t think I should be hitting him. However, I can get Bos to do for me,” she grinned.

“You’re family,” Montana said.

“You get to hit and threaten,” Indi said.

The smile on Alyssa’s face showed Jacqui just how much the words meant to Alyssa and she herself, wished she would soon be joining their loving family. Although the thought of Phoenix being ganged up on by his family was horrifying.

“No, don’t do that,” Jacqui said. “I’m sure it’s just nerves, that’s all.”

“Think about it this way. If you can get through this, then

your wedding will be a breeze," Montana said.

"Huh?" she said.

"It's true, Jacs," Indi said. "Once you've had your moment. The one where you're both honest and declaring your love for each other, everything else is simple and easy."

"I have to agree. Even with a meddling uncle and father, once Boston and I said we loved each other, nothing those two did was a big deal. Well, not for me, anyway," Alyssa giggled.

"It's like when you declare you love each other, it cements it and you both have each other's back, no matter what. That certainty is a powerful thing," Montana said.

"Yes, I've seen women hit on Jason, sometimes right in front of me," Indi said.

"Don't you get worried that he'll cheat?" Jacqui gasped.

"I know Jason would never cheat on me, especially not with those women. Sometimes, if I want great make up sex I pretend to get mad, but most of the times it just amuses me because I know we love each other. However, I do tease Jase that if a rich, young hunk comes along, I'll be having a fling," Indi giggled.

"I'll admit it was a bit of a weird thing to go from no siblings to lots where everyone knows your business," Alyssa said. "So Boston and I are always talking, to ensure he knows what I'm feeling or thinking because to him, this is all normal. That way there's no misunderstandings."

"We can all tell you about misunderstandings," Indi laughed.

"It's true, Jacs. No matter what, you and Nix have to

ensure that you keep talking to each other. That's what helps make a marriage strong," Montana said.

Jacqui began crying again, but this time it was happy tears.

"I'm so glad I met you and hope you'll become my sisters," she said.

"We are too. And, if by some weird twist of fate you two don't end up together, we'll always be your friend. *And*, we'll always be reminding Nix about what a bonehead he was to ever let you get away," Indi grinned.

Everyone laughed and it heartened Jacqui that she knew they were being sincere. She now had three new friends no matter what happened.

"But we all know you'll be our sister-in-law," Montana smiled.

"Definitely," Alyssa nodded.

"Then let's get this show on the road," Jacqui said, now more confident she was going to get her man.

"Oh, one more thing," Montana said. "You're not allowed to tell the little ones we had a spa day together."

"Why not?" she said, perplexed.

"Well, unless you want to see families at war, either say nothing or stand far, far away so you don't lose any of your body parts, especially your hearing," Indi chuckled.

"Lexi and Vanna will be in jealous fits if you say we did this without them. The accusations of being excluded blah, blah, blah will be thrown around," Montana said.

"But they're not even here, or even in the country or this hemisphere," Jacqui said, bewildered.

"Doesn't matter," Indi said, shaking her head. "They missed out and there'll be yelling and screaming."

"Wouldn't they understand since they're adults?" Jacqui said, still confused.

Everyone laughed.

"You'd think so, but maturity will fly right out the window like it never existed and we'll all revert back to our childish, younger selves," Montana laughed.

"Wow, I'm not sure if I want to see this with my own two eyes or not?" she said.

"Believe me, you don't," Alyssa giggled. "I've seen it and it's not pretty. In your mind you mistakenly used logic, but when it comes to this family, logic isn't even a consideration in their bickering. Just stand back and enjoy the show. And what's even better is now I'll have you to enjoy it with me. In fact, maybe we could give you a suit of armour as an engagement present."

"Or a big shield," Montana said.

"Okay then, I guess I'll, or we'll all keep our lips zipped," she said.

"Although…" Indi said.

"Although what?" Jacqui said, nervous.

"Sometimes the boys like to lob out grenades to start us fighting. You know, years later, we'll all be having a great time and someone will bring something up to get us fighting. They think it's hilarious," Indi said.

"Yes, but then it backfires on them because once we've calmed down, we then pile onto them and make them wish they never started it," Montana grinned.

All this information made Jacqui's mind boggle. Her relationship with Charles was nothing like what these women were telling her and she didn't know whether to be excited or terrified about joining such a family or not. However, deep down she knew as long as she had Phoenix, nothing else really mattered.

Phoenix was happy his family were all here to not only celebrate the buying of Aurora, but just to have family time with him. It meant a lot. Since the girls decided they wanted to do a spa day, it gave him time to spend with the boys where he kept repeating his thanks and they just kept laughing about it.

They had spent the morning playing golf and lunching with Tony and Trevor and that afternoon when it was just Phoenix, Boston and their brothers-in-law, he presented them with their gifts.

"It's just a little something to say thank you for all that you've done for me," he said, looking misty eyed.

"Nix, you didn't need to get us anything. We're family and would do anything for you," Boston said, looking a little teary himself.

"I agree. You've helped make us wealthier with your investment tips, so buying you a company just made sense," Jason teased.

"I concur. Hopefully now we can stop paying those exorbitant fees," Lucas chuckled.

"Doubt it," Phoenix grinned. "But I do appreciate it."

"We know, you keep telling us. None of us would have done it if we didn't think you'd be up to the job *eventually*," Boston said.

Everyone had been pleased by Trevor's observations about how Phoenix was coming along. Although he had been spooked and upset by the news that Trevor was starting to search for Jacqui's replacement, the thought of her not even being in the same building made him miserable.

"Imagined if you said you wanted us to buy you an amusement park, then we'd all be worried," Lucas chuckled.

"Yes, you'd definitely be all on your own on that one," Jason laughed.

"How about investing in one?" Phoenix grinned.

"Could be fun," Lucas smiled.

"Would we get lifetime passes for the family?" Boston said.

"Always such a cheapskate," Phoenix laughed.

He should have realised this was a set-up when the boys all said they wanted to spend quality time with their wives and would meet him at the restaurant, but because he knew what that really meant, he had taken it on face value. Now, seeing the most beautiful woman in the world standing there holding a rose, his heart stopped beating.

"Jacqui?" he said, hesitant at seeing her here in front of him looking spectacular, but it wasn't for him. She was probably on a date with Eddie, which made his stomach churn with jealousy. "What are you doing here? Are you on a date? Where's Eddie?" He hadn't wanted to ask the question, but he had to know.

"The West Coast," she smiled, unable to stop herself from giggling at his confusion. "He moved to the West Coast."

"Oh," he said, before comprehending what she was saying and brightening. "So you're not together?

"Actually I wanted to see you and ask if the names of your younger sisters are Alexandria and Savannah?" she said.

The smile that lit up his face was like sunshine.

"How did you guess?" he said.

"Let's just say I had some *sisterly* help," she smiled. "They didn't tell me their names, but their nicknames were enough of a hint. Okay, I also did kind of cheat a little and had Alyssa give me some heavy hints with Lexi's name, but that was only because I really wanted to be able to tell you them tonight. I don't think I would have ever gotten her name on my own."

He groaned.

"Now I'm sensing this is a set-up done by my meddling siblings," he said.

"Yes. Are you angry?" she said, hesitant.

"Not at you," he smiled, making her relieved. "Do I even ask how they managed to persuade you to come tonight?"

"It wasn't a knock down, drag 'em out fight, if that's what you mean. I was however, pampered until I gave in." She shyly smiled twirling the rose in her hand. "This is for you."

He smiled taking the red rose.

"And judging by the fact that we're sitting at a private table for two, we're not having a family dinner," he said, torn between being annoyed his family had tricked him and being too ecstatic to be having dinner with Jacqui to care.

"They said, they'll see us at lunch tomorrow," she smiled.

"Us?" Hope flared as fireworks of happiness exploded in his chest.

"Unless you don't want to go. I'm happy to go by myself," she teased.

"But it's my family…"

"Then I guess we have to go together."

"Together. I like that," he smiled, kissing her knowing he had finally found his one.

About the Author

Serena Black's love of reading romance novels, watching soap operas and rom-com TV shows and movies, opened her eyes to a world of romance that could be funny, adventurous, dramatic and sweet.

Now nothing makes her happier than to give readers the same bit of romantic escapism that culminates in happily ever after. No matter where her readers are, whether the day is wet and wintry or one for lazing on the beach, she hopes they pick up a book so that they might laugh, cry or even enjoy the arguments and always close the book with a loud romantic sigh.

Contact Serena at www.serenablackauthor.com.

Coming next:

Lexi's story

www.ingramcontent.com/pod-product-compliance
Lightning Source LLC
La Vergne TN
LVHW091035080826
845145LV00002B/499

* 9 7 8 0 4 7 3 7 7 4 5 8 5 *